"If I've got it, I'll have to leave, Portia."

Voicing what he'd decided—that made it real for Nelson, and he could feel the yank in his guts that said he wouldn't want to go on living without the woman next to him. The stakes had changed. His worst fear wasn't getting sick; it was losing Portia.

She was crouched on the bed, staring at him. "So you'll walk out if the lab results are positive? You'll leave me because of something that won't happen for years? You'll put me on hold and wait for some scientific test to determine how we spend the rest of our lives?"

She was trembling. He reached out a hand to smooth her arm and she knocked it away.

"You don't get it, Nelson. This is my life, right here, right now. I told you that you don't have the damn disease. It really pisses me off that you don't trust me."

"You're the one who doesn't get it. I'm trying to protect you. What the hell's wrong with you? I don't intend to ever be your patient, Portia. I want to be your husband, your lover. When I know I have time, we'll take the next step. Until then—"

She was out of bed in a flash and pulling on her clothes. "Forget *until then*. Get out, Nelson. Now. I don't feel like living in a vacuum for the next six or eight weeks or however long it takes. I'd rather be alone than on probation."

Dear Reader,

The seed for *Intensive Caring* began with the old question "How would we live our lives if we knew we had only a short time left?" Wouldn't our passion for life inevitably be intensified under such pressure? I believe the quality of joy in our lives is determined by how we spend our moments. I believe, as well, that there are rare individuals who can teach us the power of *now*, if only we have the sense to stop and listen.

Forming new relationships and being pushed to expand personal boundaries is what every romance is about, and as I wrote this one, I was reminded that none of us ever knows how long we have, how many days or months or years are left in our future to make the most of those new opportunities. Living in each moment is a tremendous challenge, because it involves enormous trust. I know, because it's a pledge I make each morning and all too often forget before noon. Those few times I've succeeded for an entire day have taught me that when we make a concerted effort to live in the now, we begin to experience life and love and relationships in a new way. And sometimes, when we're able to let go of our own plans, we find the universe rewards us, leading us on paths that we'd never on our own dare to dream possible.

I also want to illustrate that caring extends beyond the circle of a lover, or a parent or a friend. There is only one of us here; we are all brothers. Love has a power beyond our comprehension. All we have to learn is to give and receive it—unconditionally.

Thank you so much for reading my books.

With love,

Bobby

Intensive Caring
Bobby Hutchinson

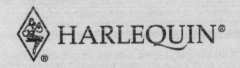

HARLEQUIN®

TORONTO • NEW YORK • LONDON
AMSTERDAM • PARIS • SYDNEY • HAMBURG
STOCKHOLM • ATHENS • TOKYO • MILAN • MADRID
PRAGUE • WARSAW • BUDAPEST • AUCKLAND

This book is for my sons, Dan, Dave and Rob Jackart.
My pride in them, my love for them,
is intensive and unlimited.

ISBN 0-373-71010-0

INTENSIVE CARING

Copyright © 2001 by Bobby Hutchinson.

ACKNOWLEDGMENT

Thank you, as always, to Patricia Gibson.
Every writer needs a muse, and you're mine, dear friend.

CHAPTER ONE

THE SEPTEMBER HEAT was breaking records for Vancouver, but self-confessed adrenaline junkie Nelson Gregory didn't even notice the sweat that soaked his body.

He was garbed in a protective electric-blue jumpsuit and strapped into an open-topped Ferrari. The acrid smell of car exhaust filled his nostrils, and streams of perspiration trickled down his neck inside the full-face helmet he also had on. Around him, race cars revved their engines to an ear-splitting scream, but Nelson barely heard them.

His gloved hands rested on the steering wheel, as the motor of his sleek and powerful Molson Indy race car thrummed its cadence matching that of the adrenaline pumping through his veins. His stomach churned and his jaw tensed as he squinted through his visor. He was waiting for the green light that in any instant would begin the race.

He'd spent the past six years honing his skills and his body to qualify for this two-hour war between his car, fondly labeled the Phoenix, and those of the other competitors in the Vancouver Indy Lights Championship Race. Heading into this meet, Nelson stood atop the drivers' standings, and he intended to win, despite his unfortunate position at the starting line.

Beneath the deafening roar from the sleek, powerful cars around him, Nelson cursed his head mechanic, Mario Lambotti.

The poor qualifying time Nelson had posted in the trials the day before meant that his start position was as bad as it could get—third to last on the starting grid. He blamed Mario for the ignominious placement.

"I need more down force," he'd insisted to Lambotti during a pit stop at the time trials the previous day. "The setup's all wrong," he'd said desperately. "Pay attention to the wings."

"We're doing our best," Lambotti had drawled. Nelson, though, had seen the sneer on his face. Lambotti wanted him to fail.

"It's you, Gregory. You're not driving the course right," the mechanic had accused.

But the issue wasn't driving, Nelson knew. It was Corinna, the sultry blonde Lambotti worshiped, who'd drunkenly declared her passion for Nelson at a party the night before the time trials. Nelson had done his best to downplay the incident, but Corinna hadn't left him much room to maneuver. She'd wound herself around him like a python, trailing her lips along his jaw, pressing her lush breasts and agile pelvis against him, and over her shoulder, Nelson had seen the frozen expression on Lambotti's face.

He should have confronted Lambotti then and there, but he'd wanted to avoid a punching match with the hot-blooded Italian. Nelson had refused to believe that his head mechanic would let personal feelings interfere with the business of racing. He'd been wrong.

Now Nelson tightened his fists on the wheel as he envisioned what he'd like to do to Lambotti's handsome features for sabotaging him in the most important race he'd ever been in—and over a woman.

Green.

Thought evaporated. Nelson brought his foot down hard on the gas pedal. The powerful car leaped ahead, accelerating to almost two hundred miles an hour within the first few minutes.

Nelson was at one with his machine, calculating his position, increasing speed, anticipating the steely ninety-degree right-hander that would come up in a moment. He concentrated on overtaking as many cars as he could before the turn.

A tiny voice warned that he was driving over his head, that at this speed he had no room for even a minuscule error. He ignored it.

As he powered his car into the tight turn, he calculated his distance from the retaining wall—and felt a thump as a car behind clipped his rear wheel.

His Ferrari swerved. He careered toward the wall, fighting with everything he had in him to regain control, aware all the while that it was hopeless—he was losing the battle.

In the final instant before he crashed, he knew that he was about to die, and even through the terror, he recognized that a weary part of him was grateful.

It would put an end to the waiting.

CHAPTER TWO

THE CHURCH WAS ALREADY crowded when Dr. Portia Bailey stepped through the huge oak doors, out of the afternoon heat and into air-conditioned coolness.

The organ was playing softly, and the silver coffin, blanketed with roses, rested at the front, just beneath the altar.

Portia felt the knot in her chest pull tighter as a black-suited usher found her a seat in a crowded pew near the back. The smells of roses and incense filled her nostrils. The sorrow hanging over the congregation fell on her shoulders like a dark, heavy cloak, weighing her down, making it difficult to breathe.

The service began.

"Saying goodbye to a loved one is always painful," the elderly pastor intoned in a sonorous voice. "Betty Hegard was a beautiful young woman, and that makes our farewell to her on this lovely autumn day even more painful, because we can't help but think that Betty should have enjoyed many more sunny days in her life.''

The words were like arrows shot straight into Portia's heart. Betty had been her patient, but the girl had also considered Portia her friend.

Betty's untimely death had raised both personal and professional issues in Portia's life. Just yesterday afternoon, the review board at St. Joseph's Medical Center, where Portia was completing her residency, had looked into Betty's death and concluded that Portia had made a serious error of judgment in treating the young woman.

As an asthmatic, Betty had relied on highly addictive steroids to control her condition. Portia had suggested that Betty address some emotional components of the condition and try to cut down on medication. Instead of cutting down, Betty had stopped using the inhalers entirely. She died of a massive heart attack, a common side effect of stopping steroids too quickly.

The hospital review board would take no disciplinary action, but it had severely reprimanded Portia for giving a patient the wrong advice.

Choking back tears now, she sat through the service. When it was over, she joined the subdued mourners as they filed slowly out of the church into the brilliant sunlight.

"You. Dr. Bailey. How dare you show your face at my daughter's funeral?"

The angry words came from behind Portia, startling her. She jerked around to face Betty's mother. The short, heavy woman, her eyes swollen from crying, rushed over, her plump, florid face twisted into a grimace of what felt to Portia like absolute hatred.

For one awful moment, Portia thought Mrs. Hegard was about to assault her, but she stopped a few inches away and shook her finger under Portia's nose.

"You killed my daughter. You have no right to come to her funeral," Mrs. Hegard raged. She burst into hysterical tears. "Get her out of here," she howled. "I never want to see her again." Her voice rose to a shriek. "She's the reason my Betty's dead. Telling my darling girl not to take her medication... What kind of doctor does a thing like that?"

Portia, shocked speechless by the attack, stood frozen for one long, horrified moment. Then, knowing every eye was on her, she turned with what dignity she could muster and walked down the crowded street toward the car park. Her legs felt like sponges. Her face was burning. Her hands shook violently as she tried to unlock her car. It wasn't until she managed finally to crawl into the driver's seat and slam the door that she realized she was murmuring over and over in a monotone voice that didn't even sound like her, ''I didn't tell her to stop. I didn't. I didn't.''

Near panic made her entire body tremble.

She drew on will and a relaxation technique to control it—a pattern of breathing that she'd learned from a fellow intern years before—and at last she was able to insert the key into the ignition, start the motor, pay the car park attendant and drive to St. Joseph's Medical Center.

Portia pulled into the employees' parking lot behind St. Joe's and hurried through the labyrinthine passageways that led to the emergency room, praying that she'd be too busy for the next twelve hours to think about Mrs. Hegard's hurtful accusations, or Betty's untimely death.

She was late for her shift, but Joanne Mathews had promised to cover for her. Joanne was her mentor, her closest friend. For an instant, Portia imagined throwing herself into the older woman's arms and giving in to a flood of agonizing tears. But of course she wouldn't. She couldn't, not at work. Professional conduct forbade such behavior.

She pushed through the doors to the ER and grabbed a set of green scrubs from a metal laundry cart before she headed into the women's locker room. There she quickly took off the tailored gray dress, panty hose and heels she'd worn for the funeral. She donned the scrubs and a pair of comfortable flats, noting that her hands were still trembling a little.

In the employees' lounge, Olivia Jenkins, the cheerful new ER nurse, was boiling water in the microwave for a cup of tea to go with her tuna sandwich.

"Hey, Doc Bailey, how's it goin'?"

Olivia's smile was impossible to resist. It lit up her otherwise plain features and demanded a response.

"Great," Portia lied, forcing a smile in return. "What's shaking out there?"

"Same old crowd." Olivia grinned. "Some of our weekend regulars have been in. Other than that it hasn't been too busy yet, which makes me think it's the calm before the hurricane. Doc Mathews is in three with a motor vehicle accident from the Indy race. One of the drivers smacked into a retaining wall. He was the only one injured. The Emergency Response Team brought him in about forty minutes ago."

Portia vaguely remembered having heard about the accident on the car radio as she'd driven to the hospital from the funeral, but she'd been too distracted to pay much attention.

"Is he local or from out of town?" She knew the Indy had brought cars and drivers from all over the world to Vancouver, but beyond that, the race was a mystery.

"Local guy. No immediate relatives, though. Three of his crew are in the waiting room. He didn't want us to call anybody else. Like some tea? I can easily heat up another cupful."

"No, thanks," Portia said. "I've gotta hustle. I'm late." She hurried out, automatically gauging the activity in the ER.

Just as Olivia had indicated, this afternoon there was a definite lull in the usual frantic pace. An intern was chatting with the triage nurse, and Portia greeted them as she made her way to the desk to check in.

Only two of the examination cubicles were in use. No one was bellowing for attention, and the waiting area, too often overflowing with anxious relatives, was empty except for the three young men from the race. They were easy to identify—all were wearing brightly colored coveralls with the Indy logo.

Portia made her way to trauma room three to let Joanne know she was back and to see if she could be of assistance with the MVA—motor vehicle accident—but a glance told her that here, too, things were under control. The medical team surrounding the bed were focused, but their intensity wasn't extreme. Obviously the critical stage was over with.

"Hi, Portia." Joanne Mathews left the patient's

side and came over to the door. "How'd it go?" she asked, her voice pitched low, her green eyes showing her concern.

She knew Portia had attended Betty's funeral. Joanne had been wonderfully supportive during the crisis surrounding Betty's death.

"Not good. I'll fill you in later." Portia swallowed hard at the painful memory. "Thanks for covering for me. What's the status here?"

"Nelson Gregory, thirty-six, race car driver. Hit a wall. Jammed his feet against the floorboards. Fractured heels on both feet. Fractured right fibula. Dislocated hip. Extensive bruising to the chest and abdomen. No internal bleeding. Possible spinal damage—the initial X rays were nonconfirmatory. Because of the pain and the spasms he's experiencing, we'll do a bone scan in a day or two. What do you think?"

The first thing Portia thought was that after Betty died she'd promised herself never again to use the special ability she had to diagnose a patient.

But she couldn't explain that to Joanne now. Her friend was asking her for a favor, and she couldn't refuse.

She looked past Joanne at the strong torso of the man on the table. He was naked except for a sheet over his groin. He was obviously an athlete. Beneath the tubes and medical paraphernalia that surrounded him, he had a lean, well-muscled and well-toned body. His face and arms were deeply tanned; his thick, curly black hair was now wet with sweat. He wore a breathing mask, and a collar to protect his spine. He was conscious.

The room was small, and Portia allowed herself to become viscerally aware of the pain and fear he was experiencing. She scanned him, noting the injuries that Joanne had mentioned. They showed up clearly as breaks in the swirl of colors surrounding him. Portia looked for the disruption in his aura that would tell her his spinal cord was damaged.

It wasn't there.

"He has no serious injury to the spine that I can see," she told Joanne in a definite tone. "He's probably just got whiplash."

She'd spoken quietly, yet she intuitively knew the patient had heard her. Because of the cervical collar, he couldn't move his head, but his blue eyes darted frantically, searching for her.

Portia moved closer so she could meet his gaze. She smiled down at him. "Just try to relax now, Mr. Gregory. It'll make your breathing easier. Your injuries are painful, but you're going to come through this absolutely intact." She grinned at him and winked. "Trust me." She moved back to allow the trauma team to do their job.

"No spinal injury—that's a big relief."

Joanne didn't ask how Portia knew. Neither did she question her certainty. They'd worked together for four years, and Joanne had witnessed the accuracy of Portia's unique and unorthodox diagnostic methods innumerable times. Joanne trusted Portia's conclusions even though she didn't fully understand how Portia arrived at them. For that unquestioning trust, Portia was profoundly grateful. Particularly today. If ever she'd needed reassurance, it was now.

"You want me to take over in here so you can head home?" Joanne had toddlers, Lillianna and Benjamin, adorable three-year-old twins with jade-green eyes, curly black hair and formidable energy.

"No rush. I've actually got the day to myself. Lillian and Bud are visiting. They've taken the kids to the park for the afternoon, and Spence is making dinner for everyone. I'll stick around until Mr. Gregory goes up to the OR."

Lillian was Joanne's mother-in-law, one of the most vibrant older women Portia had ever met.

"Tell Lillian I said hi. If it stays this quiet, maybe you and I can grab a coffee before you leave?"

"I'd like that. I want to hear about the funeral."

Portia blew out a breath and shook her head, but before she could say anything, the door behind them swung open and Olivia stuck her head in. "Doc Bailey, could you come and have a look at this patient? Kid's fourteen. Looks to me like she's having a grand mal seizure. Her mother says there's no history, though.''

''I'll be right there. See you later, Joanne.'' Portia hurried off to begin her twelve-hour shift.

NELSON WAS AWARE that she'd left the room. Other voices buzzed around him like a swarm of friendly bees, but hers, clear, confident and soothing, was missing.

They'd given him something to dull the agonizing pain in his lower body, but it hadn't made him sleepy yet. Instead, he was hyperconscious, intensely aware of everything that was happening.

He'd blacked out after the crash, then woken to a cacophony of frightened voices and the ongoing scream of powerful engines still circling the track. The foul odor of burning rubber and the acrid stench of foam had assaulted him as firemen and first-aid attendants surrounded him. At first, he'd had no sensation except stunned surprise that he was still alive. And then red-hot pain consumed him, the most intense pain he'd ever known. He couldn't get his breath. His lungs were on fire. He'd needed every ounce of self-control to keep from weeping, before, mercifully, he'd lost consciousness again.

When he'd awoke in the ambulance, strapped to a board, an oxygen mask covering his nose and making it marginally easier to breathe, the indescribable torment in his legs was nearly beyond bearing. That was when it came to him that he must have hopelessly mangled his feet; he knew that jamming the legs against the floorboards of a race car caused extreme injuries. Would his lower legs have to be amputated? The suspicion had sent icy fear through every cell.

He'd tried to ask the young medic in the ambulance, but his voice wouldn't work. He couldn't get enough air in his lungs to produce more than a garbled moan. In abject terror and unspeakable agony, he'd endured the transfer from the ambulance to this room. He'd thought so often the past few years that death would be a friend if it came quickly and unexpectedly. But living with no feet was a horror beyond imagining.

Dr. Mathews had taken charge the moment he'd arrived at St. Joe's. She'd asked questions, explained each procedure as it was performed and reassured him when he gasped out his concern about his feet.

There was no question of amputation, she'd said, but his heels were badly fractured, along with the long outer bone on his lower right leg. His right hip was also dislocated. The fact that he was feeling so much pain was a good sign, she'd told him, but not a guarantee that the accident hadn't damaged his spinal column.

Damaged his spine? The relief over his legs gave way to a renewed panic as the medical team inserted needles into his arms, asked him still more questions, rolled machines into place and positioned his limbs for X rays. His body seemed to have a capacity for pain he'd never dreamed possible.

And then he'd heard Dr. Mathews talking to someone she called Portia, obviously also a doctor. He heard the swift recitation of his injuries, the note of concern in Mathews's tone when she mentioned his spine, the relief in her voice when Portia assured her there was no permanent damage.

He didn't question how the woman called Portia knew. She had such confidence that he simply believed what she said, and his own relief was overwhelming. Even through the paroxysms of pain he was able to relax marginally. When the owner of the voice came close enough for him to see her, he wanted to thank her, as though she'd given him an invaluable gift with her assurances.

He still couldn't speak clearly, but he looked up at her, and as if taking a mental snapshot, he memorized the unusual angularity of her face, the opaque grayness of her eyes, the wild spikiness of her short black hair.

She smiled and winked at him, then told him firmly that he would be fine.

Her utter confidence calmed him as he was taken

to the operating room. His last thought before the anesthesia guided him down to a dark and timeless space was of the woman named Portia.

"IT GOT BUSY THERE for a while, but it's slacked off again." Portia stirred a heaping spoonful of sugar into her mug of tea and sank back into the rumpsprung sofa. "How's your Indy driver doing?"

The staff lounge was empty except for her and Joanne, and the two women slumped comfortably side by side, feet up on the battered coffee table.

"He's still in surgery. Before it goes nuts again out there, tell me about the funeral this morning," Joanne said. "What the heck happened? You looked as if you'd been whipped when you got back."

Portia shuddered at the memory. She took a gulp of hot tea and swore when it burned her mouth. Then she carefully described the painful scene with Betty's mother.

"She screamed at me with everyone listening, ordered me to leave, said I had no right to be there. She believes I was totally responsible for her daughter's death."

"That's absolutely ridiculous." Joanne snorted. "I've never understood why people have to blame someone when a loved one dies. Particularly a doctor who'd done everything in her power to keep the patient alive."

"Maybe so, but Mrs. Hegard isn't alone in thinking I made a mistake with Betty," Portia commented. "The hospital review board reprimanded me, as well, remember."

"Yeah, well, in my opinion you oughta demand an apology from them. Betty Hegard was an asthmatic who relied totally on inhalers and was doing herself serious damage by overusing them," Joanne reminded Portia forcefully. "We all know that inhalers are effective for flare-ups. Using them the way Betty did worsens the asthma and increases the possibility of death from an attack. All you did was sensibly suggest she cut down on them and try some alternative therapies for controlling her disease, right?"

Portia sighed. "Yes, but that wasn't all of it." What a relief it was to unburden herself to Joanne. "When I looked at Betty, I could clearly see the reasons for her chronic asthma. I used my intuitive abilities instead of following standard medical procedure, and I suggested she explore the underlying emotional components of her physical illness—an early abortion that Betty never stopped grieving for or feeling guilty about."

"How did you know? Did she tell you?"

Portia nodded. "I could see that the energy in her pelvis was blocked, and one day she broke down and told me why. It revealed so much about her, about the reasons behind her ups and downs. I suggested she talk to someone. I knew that her emotions were keeping her sick, making her attacks more frequent and more severe. And yes, I suggested she cut back on the puffers, explaining that they were highly addictive.'' Portia frowned, trying to remember the exact sequence of events.

"I'm sure I told her to do it slowly. I never dreamed she'd interpret what I said to mean she should stop using them overnight. She'd been on them long enough to know all the risks. I'm pretty sure she did it deliberately, and that's what I feel the worst about—not recognizing that she was suicidal.''

"Stop it.'' Joanne's voice was stern. "The girl was clearly far more disturbed than anyone realized,'' she declared. "You weren't the only doctor treating her. Her family physician had as much or more responsibility for her welfare as you did.''

"Betty idolized me, Joanne.'' Portia struggled to keep the ready tears at bay. "She was in Emerg so many times this past six months I got to know her really well. I knew she was emotionally unstable and I did suggest she get psychiatric help—some counseling, at the very least—but maybe I wasn't as insistent as I should have been.''

"We can't always force patients to do what's best for them,'' Joanne reminded her. "She certainly wasn't psychotic enough to be admitted. And you told me Betty's mother tore a strip off you that time you advised counseling for her daughter. Which is probably why the woman was so abusive to you today—she knows now she should have listened. Guilt is what made her turn on you. It's easier to blame you than to accept some of that blame herself."

Joanne looked at Portia and her voice softened. "But none of this really helps, does it? The simple fact is you lost a patient and you feel horrible about it. I know all about that. Nothing anyone says makes it easier."

Portia felt tears start to flow, and she swiped at them with the back of her hand. "We both know what the real issue is, Joanne."

She had to struggle to keep her voice from trembling. "I used my psychic ability with Betty. I did it again just now with your racing driver, even though I vowed when Betty died I'd never do it again. I can shut the ability off if I choose. It's hard, but I can do it. Yet when I'm confronted with severely injured or desperately ill individuals, it's so tempting to read their auras. I can see where things are going wrong, how bad they are."

"And you always do the scientific tests to back up what you intuit," Joanne pointed out quickly.

Portia nodded. She was scrupulous about that.

"Still, using my psychic talents with Betty was a huge mistake. I can't stop thinking that if I'd just followed standard procedures and left things at that, she might still be alive."

"Hindsight's always twenty-twenty." Joanne reached over and with a soothing hand rubbed the younger woman's shoulder. "I've relied on your psychic ability more often than I can count, and I've never known you to be wrong. You've got to think of all the lives you've saved by trusting your gift."

Portia realized that Joanne was doing everything in her power to make her feel better. She wouldn't for the world hurt her friend by admitting it wasn't helping, despite the unforgiving knot in the pit of her stomach that just wouldn't go away.

So she made a concerted effort to lighten the atmosphere.

"I know how often I've told you I'm staying single, but I have to confess that at times like this I wish to God I had a partner, Joanne. Just some sweet, undemanding, caring guy who wouldn't freak when he found out I saw rainbows around everybody."

"He's at the end of a rainbow waiting for you to find him," Joanne teased. "It's like real estate—location, location, location. He's probably right under your nose, waiting to be noticed."

"I'd laugh at that if it hadn't happened to you."

Joanne had met Spence right here at St. Joe's. He'd been a security guard. Now he owned and operated the largest security company in Vancouver. Their romance had given Portia much-needed reassurance about love and marriage.

"I feel blessed to have Spence in my life." Joanne grinned. "Although at moments I feel both blessed *and* beleaguered, what with the twins and my job and his business. Remember, too, he didn't come along until I was forty-one. You've got a lot bigger window of opportunity than I had to locate Mr. Right. For heaven's sake, you're still a girl, my friend."

"Some girl." Portia rolled her eyes. "Twenty-eight, turning twenty-nine in a couple months, and great guys sure aren't lining up to date me." Portia sighed dramatically. "Sometimes I think I must have been born without the romance gene. My mother can't understand what's wrong with me. She keeps reminding me she'd been married twice by the time she was my age."

"Quality, Portia. Think quality. With all due respect to your mother, marriage isn't about quantity. By the way, what happened to that hunk of a radiologist you were seeing? Tom…was that his name?"

"Todd." Portia shrugged. "I got tired of hearing about the legal battles he went through with his ex.

He was hanging on to the anger and resentment as though they were annuities, for cripes' sake. I started sympathizing out loud with her instead of him. For some strange reason he got upset about that. So I had to fire him.''

Joanne was still laughing when the intercom blared, ''Dr. Bailey, please report to Emerg—stat. Dr. Bailey to Emerg.''

Portia drained her tea and got to her feet. ''Back to the battleground. Give those little angels of yours kisses from me.''

''Shall do, although *angels* isn't the term I'd use for them,'' Joanne said, but she couldn't disguise the pride in her tone.

''See you soon, Joanne. You working next week?''

''Tuesday and Friday.'' Since the birth of the twins, Joanne had given up her position as senior ER physician. She came in now on a casual basis, so she could spend as much time as possible with her babies and her husband.

''I'm on shift both days.'' Portia hurried back to the ER, where the triage nurse informed her a teenage male with severe gunshot wounds would be arriving in seven minutes.

Portia pulled on protective clothing, sterile gloves and glasses, and as the attendants hurried through the outside port to trauma room one with a stretcher bearing a screaming and bloody young boy named Saul, every personal thought disappeared.

Here was someone needing everything Portia could give. And in that total giving was solace, because there was neither time nor energy to think about anything except keeping a foolish sixteen-year-old from bleeding out. She did, however, make a conscious effort to avoid studying his aura. She'd promised herself she'd stop using it with her patients, and from now on, she was, by God, going to do her best to keep that promise.

CHAPTER THREE

PORTIA WAS ON DUTY AGAIN two afternoons later when one of the nurses from the surgical ward on the fourth floor sought her out in Emerg.

"Dr. Bailey, do you have a minute? I'm Bridget Reiss. I have a patient who's asking for you. His name's Nelson Gregory. I told him I'd pass along the message."

In spite of the dozens of patients she'd seen in the past forty-eight hours, Portia remembered him well.

"The race car driver."

"Right. He's very insistent."

"Did he say why?"

Bridget shook her blond head and shrugged. "He probably just wants to thank you for caring for him in Emerg."

"I didn't treat him. He was Doc Mathews's patient. How's he doing, anyway?"

"Came through surgery fine—he's really physically fit, which always helps. The bone scan confirmed that his spine is uninjured, which is a real blessing. His feet are in casts. He's also in a hip brace. Pretty major injuries, but I guess you've gotta be suicidal in the first place to drive one of those racing cars.''

"Isn't that the truth. Well, he's looking at a long convalescence,'' Portia remarked. "Hospital at least a couple of weeks, in a wheelchair for about six. Then it'll take months before he's really mobile again.''

Bridget nodded. "Extensive physio, too. That type of injury is pretty debilitating. He seems like an okay guy, although you can tell he's used to getting what he wants when he wants it. Or doesn't want it—apparently a young woman came to visit him yesterday and he had Security escort her out. She was pretty upset...caused quite an uproar. She sure had an interesting vocabulary.'' Bridget grinned.

"Gregory sounds like a prima donna to me.''

"I guess money'll do that. He told one of the nurses he's a commodities broker—the racing is just a sideline. But those cars cost a fortune. You gotta be loaded to get into racing. That's what my boyfriend says. Anyway, Doctor, I'll tell him I passed the message along.''

"Thanks.'' Portia smiled and went off to find her next patient.

It was Cedric Vencouer, a man she'd gotten to

know well over the years and for whom she had a
great deal of affection. He was a street person, and
he'd been coming in every few months ever since
she was an intern. Over the years Portia had treated
him for complications related to drinking. For the
past year, he'd fought to stop using drugs. He'd
been successful, and he'd told her the last time she'd
seen him that he'd also cut down on alcohol.

As a result, his complaints now were usually minor, sometimes real, sometimes imagined. His de-
votion to Portia had caused much amusement
among the staff; they teased her for attracting unusual groupies.

Cedric had been friends with another skid-row
derelict named Abner, who'd also refused to have
any doctor care for him but Portia. Abner had died
a year ago from a drug overdose, and that sad event
had impelled Cedric's sobriety.

The nurses all knew Cedric. They knew he'd wait
patiently, sometimes for hours, until Portia was free.
Today he sat perched on an examination table in
one of the curtained cubicles. He always had a dis-
tinctive scent about him, which the nurses labeled
eau de skid row. He usually wore layers of sweaters
and shirts, with a battered ski jacket overtop, no
matter the season. His jeans were clean, but worn
paper thin.

Chronologically, he was young, but the years on

the streets had taken their toll. Many of his teeth were gone, and he looked years older than thirty-eight, with deep trenches carved into hollow cheeks. When he saw her, a wide blissful smile transformed his rugged face, and his deep-set green eyes danced with pleasure.

"Cedric." Portia smiled back at him. She so much admired his struggle to stay free of drugs and remain sober. In spite of his lifestyle, he had something innocent and endearing about him that had always touched her heart.

"Hello, my friend." She took his right hand in hers the way she always did, noting that today his fingers didn't curl around her own. She felt him make the effort, but the hand didn't cooperate. "I haven't seen you for a while. How are you?"

"'She is too fair, too wise; wisely too fair.'" He always greeted her with a line of poetry, always different, always flattering, but today his voice was slurred and barely above a whisper.

"You got me. Where's it from?" It was a game they played.

"Romeo and Juliet," he explained with a winsome grin.

Cedric could quote poetry and lines from songs endlessly, and normally his rich tenor voice was arresting. He'd never told Portia much about his background, other than insisting he had no living relatives, but if his use of language and his knowledge of the classics were any indication, he'd had a better-than-average education.

"Okay, Romeo. What can I do for you today?" She was assessing him silently, dismissing the possibility that he might be drunk. There was no odor of liquor.

He frowned and rubbed his shoulder. "I think I've got a pinched nerve or something, Doc Bailey. My right side doesn't have any strength anymore."

"Just your hand?"

He shook his head. "My leg, too. I fell over my own feet a couple times last week."

"How long since you first noticed this weakness?"

"Maybe a month now. My back's been hurting more than usual. I kept thinking the pain would go away, but instead it got lots worse this past week."

Portia began some basic muscle testing, trying to ignore the foreboding that overtook her as it became obvious Cedric's right arm, shoulder, leg and hip were discernibly weak.

He chatted while she assessed him.

"How's the real-life Juliet, Doc?"

"She's fine. She's staying with me next weekend." Juliet was Portia's younger sister, who'd been born mentally challenged. Portia had told Cedric about her one day, and now he always asked about her.

"She likes where she's living?"

"Very much. And she enjoys her job, as well." For the past several years, Juliet had been living in a group home and working in a bakery.

"Good for her. Tell her Cedric says hi."

"I'll do that." Portia finished her examination and helped him get his shirt on. He couldn't button it, so she did it for him.

"Thanks. So what's the verdict, Doc Portia?"

"I'm not exactly sure, Cedric. Muscles can become weak for many reasons. We have to figure out whether muscle function is abnormal because there's a disease of the muscle itself, or whether a disorder has developed in other tissue."

He frowned at her and shook his head. "What other tissue?"

"Nerve tissue." Neuromuscular disease was often genetic. "Do you know anything at all about your mother or father, Cedric, whether they might have had any physical problems?"

"My mother abandoned me in the pew of a church when I was about a year old. I have no idea who she was—or my father, either."

Cedric's tone was matter-of-fact. He'd learned to accept the facts of his life, but the information tugged at Portia's heart.

"I think we need to admit you so I can run some tests," she said. Pronounced muscular weakness, pain in the shoulder, falling—Cedric's symptoms suggested a serious neuromuscular disorder.

At the mention of admission, his smile faded and he shook his head vehemently. "Can't do that, Doc. You know I can't abide hospitals. Can't stand being closed in."

"It won't be for long, Cedric," she coaxed. "I need to find out exactly what's causing this so I know how to help you. It won't be for one hour longer than you need," she assured him. She remembered how he'd told her, when she'd once suggested she admit him to treat an infection in his foot, that hospitals felt like prisons to him, and the only reason he came to St. Joe's was to see her.

"What sort of tests?"

"An EMG—electromyogram—to find out whether the nerve controlling the muscle activity in your right side is functioning normally. An MRI—magnetic resonance imaging. And some serum enzyme tests to measure the amount of muscle protein present in your blood."

He screwed up his face and shuddered dramatically. "Needles. I hate needles."

"Everybody does, and I won't order any more tests than are absolutely necessary, I promise."

He sat in silence for several moments.

"Do you figure this is something serious, Doc Portia?" He looked straight into her eyes, and she prayed her own anxiety didn't show.

"I hope not, but there's no way of telling until I get the test results."

He sighed and, with great reluctance, agreed to be admitted. "For a couple of days. That's it. After a couple of days I check out of this hotel. Deal, Doc?"

"You're not giving me much choice, so I guess it'll have to be enough." Arranging for the tests she had in mind would take longer than a couple of days, but she'd do her best to hurry things up.

"Will you come up to the ward with me? I have these etchings I know you'd love to see." Cedric made the request playful and flirtatious, but Portia understood how apprehensive he was.

"Of course. Just wait here a minute. I'll make sure there's space and be right back for you."

Fortunately, a bed was available. When she got back to where Cedric waited, she could see how difficult walking was for him. She realized he would hate being taken up in a wheelchair, so she ambled beside him to the elevators, hoping he wouldn't fall.

"I spent years in a place like this. You'd think this would feel like home," Cedric grumbled as the elevator rose slowly to the fourth floor.

"You were in a hospital as a child?"

He shook his head. "It was a boys' home, but it smelled just like this place—of disinfectant and fear. I ran away when I was ten."

"Being on your own at such an early age must have been terribly hard for you." It was almost impossible to imagine how he'd survived.

"I managed. Then I did what every kid dreams of—I ran off with the circus."

"You never told me that before."

"It wasn't much of a life, although I made a couple good friends. That's where I met Abner. And one of the clowns, Ricardo. He'd been an actor. He got me started reading."

The elevator stopped and Portia led the way to the nursing station. She knew the nurse on duty, and the kind older woman smiled warmly and assured her that Cedric would get her personal attention.

Portia left him in her care. Her heart was heavy as she made her way back down the long hallway. She couldn't shake her premonition that Cedric's tests wouldn't be positive, although—as with the teenage boy—she'd carefully avoided looking at him with the intention of seeing what was wrong. The race car driver had been the last.

Nelson Gregory was on the same floor as Cedric, in the surgical wing, she remembered. She decided on the spur of the moment to drop in on him. The ER knew where she was; they'd page her if necessary. She'd stay only a moment, she assured herself, just long enough to find out what he wanted.

He was in room 482, a private room. The door was ajar, and the sound of male voices told her he had visitors.

Portia hesitated, then pushed the door open.

The first thing she noticed was the flowers. They were everywhere...on the bedside stand, the windowsill, beside the sink, even on the floor...huge hothouse bouquets of roses, carnations, lilies. Gregory was obviously popular.

The second thing she noted was that he was extremely attractive, even with his hair matted from the pillow and his jaw covered with several days' growth of stubby dark whiskers.

His eyes, deep set beneath thick dark brows, were an arresting blue. His large, slightly crooked nose had been broken at some point. His mouth was long and sensually narrow, his jawline firm and well defined.

A young man and an older one sat on either side of the hospital bed, and both got quickly to their feet when she came in.

"Hello, Mr. Gregory." She smiled at him and nodded to his visitors.

"Dr. Bailey. Thank you for coming." His voice was still weak, but it, too, was pleasing...deep and clear.

"These are members of my pit crew, Jake Nash and Andy Wallis. Dr. Portia Bailey."

The men nodded and extended their hands, and Portia shook each in turn. "Please, sit down," she urged them. "I can only stay a moment."

Jake glanced at the man in the bed and obviously some signal passed between them. "We gotta be going. We'll see you later, Nelson. Nice to meet you, Doctor."

They hurried out. The door sighed shut behind them, and suddenly Portia felt awkward. Injured or not, Nelson Gregory exuded a male charisma that made her uneasy. She handled it by being ultraprofessional.

"You're looking very well, Mr. Gregory. The nurse said you wanted to see me. How may I be of help to you?"

"Call me Nelson, for starters. And I wanted to thank you for what you did for me in Emergency."

Portia frowned. "I'm afraid you have me confused with Dr. Mathews. I didn't treat you. She did."

"I know that, and I'm also grateful to her. But it was your reassurance that made such a difference to me. I heard you tell her that my back wasn't injured, and then you leaned over the bed and told me that I'd come through everything just fine. I did, and you were right about my back."

Portia smiled at him and said lightly, "It must have been a lucky guess."

"It didn't sound like a guess to me. How did you know?"

His intelligent eyes searched her face, and it was all she could do not to look away.

His arms were bare beneath the short-sleeved hospital gown, muscular and covered with dark hair. For an instant she remembered how his body had appeared in the ER...sinewy, strong, dusted with the same dark pelt. Another wave of awareness of him as a man brought color to her face, and the resulting embarrassment made her feel uncomfortably warm.

What's wrong with you, Bailey? He's a patient. You're a doctor. Get a grip.

Some treacherous little voice insisted, *Not* his *doctor, though.*

She needed to be very firm with herself. "I'm a doctor," she stated, more for her own benefit than his. "It's part of my job to make patients feel optimistic about the outcome of their treatment."

"But you were so confident, so certain," he insisted. "You knew somehow that my spine wasn't injured. How did you know?"

This was a slippery slope, and she didn't want to traverse it. She turned the question back on him.

"As I said, it must have been a lucky guess. Why not leave it at that."

He studied her for a long moment, and then he nodded. "Luck. You're right. That's what it was. Guess I'm just not accustomed to getting lucky." He gave her a mischievous grin. "The whole thing stuck in my head because you were like a guardian angel or something, coming in and telling me I would be okay just when I needed most to hear it. And afterward I wondered if maybe I'd just imagined you."

Portia laughed. "Me, a guardian angel? Not a chance. I'm plain old flesh and blood, same as everyone else."

"Not the same at all. Much more beautiful."

The compliment came easily to him. *He's sweet-talked a lot of women, this guy.* Her tone when she replied was deliberately flippant. "Thank you, kind sir. And now I really have to be getting back to the ER."

She was moving toward the door, but his voice stopped her.

"How long before they'll let me up?"

"I suspect you'll be in a wheelchair fairly soon, probably in another day or two." She knew he was stalling to keep her there. He must have already asked his own doctor that question.

He blew out his breath in an exasperated whoosh.

"Lying in this damn bed is making me nuts. I'm bad-tempered, and I don't mean to be. It's just being so bloody helpless that does it."

The harsh honesty of his words roused her sympathy. "I believe it. I'd hate that, too. My worst thing is forced inactivity."

"Mine, too. Besides, I need to be mobile because I want to take you out to dinner. You are single, aren't you?"

His directness took her totally by surprise, even though she was accustomed to having males come on to her.

She smiled at him and shook her head. "Thank you, Mr. Gregory, but that's not possible. There are strict rules about doctors dating patients."

"Please, call me Nelson," he told her again. "And that rule only applies if a doctor is actively engaged in a patient's treatment. All you did was talk to me. You weren't involved in treating me. You said so yourself. So there's no patient-doctor complication, is there?"

She had to laugh. He was clever. "You sound as if you checked it out with our legal department."

"I did."

"You're not serious." His admission stunned her. She'd been joking, but obviously he was in earnest.

"Of course I am. I believe in being thorough. You are single, aren't you? Otherwise you'd have used that excuse instead of the doctor-patient thing. Do you mind if I call you Portia?''

He was outrageous, and a small part of her did mind. Using her given name implied an intimacy that she wasn't ready for. But refusing would make her sound like a total prude.

''Not at all.'' She wouldn't be seeing him again, anyway, she told herself. The guy was probably a human steamroller when he wasn't confined to a hospital bed.

''Portia.''

The way he said it was seductive, which was ridiculous. His legs were in casts. His hip was in a brace. He was flat on his back. And certainly she'd never found injured patients seductive in the least.

''It's an unusual name. Shakespearean?''

The question reminded her of Cedric, and her duties as a doctor. ''Yeah. My mother's a big fan of the Bard. And now I really do have to go. Bye, Mr. Gregory.''

''Nelson.'' His eyes twinkled, but his voice was insistent. ''See you soon, Portia. I'll be in touch.''

She had to laugh. Nelson Gregory was sure of himself; she'd give him that. As she hurried down the hall to the elevator and rode back down to Emerg, she wondered how many of the floral bouquets in his room were from women he'd used and discarded.

Probably all of them.

THE DOOR SIGHED SHUT behind her, and Nelson exhaled and consciously relaxed the tight muscles in his arms and back. She made him feel like a sweaty-palmed teenager. Years had passed since he'd felt nervous around a woman, but he felt that way around Portia. It had something to do with those eyes of hers, gray laser beams that could bore a hole right through a man's soul.

He also felt horny as hell, which was surprising, considering his injuries, but also reassuring to his male ego. She was a huge challenge, and if ever he needed a challenge, it was now.

Given the sorry state his body was in, having a physical relationship with her would be difficult, but he'd figure out a way. He was powerfully attracted to her, although he knew any relationship they had would be short-lived and superficial; he never allowed himself to care too much for any woman.

Planning the seduction would give his mind a focus, though, during the endless nights trapped in this bed. Since the accident, he'd had to use every morsel of self-control to keep from going mad. For many years, he'd relied on physical activity, extreme danger, casual sex, to keep himself from thinking, to exhaust himself so totally that sleep would come easily, getting him through the worst of the dark night hours. The crash had changed all that.

Even now, in broad daylight, he broke into a sweat at the prospect of the coming night. His medications wore off long before dawn, and he'd lie trapped in the semidarkness, unable to move, listening to sirens wailing on Burrard Street, hearing ambulances pulling in and out of the hospital bays far below. And every minute, every second, he'd struggle—and fail—to keep his mind from the monstrous thing that obsessed it.

Huntington's chorea, his traitorous brain related, as if he was reading the definition from a medical encyclopedia, *a hereditary, incurable disease of the central nervous system, which involves the degeneration of nerve cells in the largest portion of the brain, known as the cerebrum.*

Nelson had firsthand experience with the disease. He'd watched his father slowly succumb to it. An only child, he'd idolized his strong, loving father. To watch the person he knew and adored slowly disappear had been a living nightmare.

The irony was that until Nelson was twenty-four, he had never heard of Huntington's. The fact that it had ravaged his father's family for generations had been a closely guarded secret. But when his father developed the unmistakable symptoms, of course Nelson had to be told.

He remembered as if it were yesterday, sitting in the doctor's comfortable office, hearing facts that had irrevocably changed his life.

"The first symptoms of Huntington's usually begin between thirty-five and forty years of age," the weary-looking doctor had explained with a regretful sigh. "As you see with your father, Nelson, the disease affects bodily movements, intellectual functioning and emotional control. The child of a person with HC has a fifty-percent chance of inheriting it. More males contract it than do females. At the moment, there is no test that can determine whether or not you have inherited the gene, although researchers are working to that end."

And then in 1993, scientists announced the discovery of a gene test to predict Huntington's chorea before symptoms developed. Nelson couldn't bring himself to have it then, and he had no desire to have it now.

There was no cure for the disease. Taking the test would only verify what he knew deep in his soul. He carried the gene. He was doomed; it was only a matter of time. Why bother having it confirmed?

The flowers his friends had sent suddenly reminded Nelson of his father's funeral, when instead of sorrow all he'd felt was overwhelming relief that the horror was over. He jabbed the call button.

A nurse came hurrying in, and he waved at the

floral tributes. ''Take these out of here. Give 'em to whoever wants them. The smell is making me nauseous.''

He closed his eyes as the nurse removed the flowers, and concentrated hard on exactly how he would go about seducing Dr. Portia Bailey.

CHAPTER FOUR

PORTIA BURIED HER NOSE in the bouquet of wild
roses beside Cedric's bed. She'd thought before she
came in to see him that she had her emotions under
control, but the fear and dread in his eyes were so
evident it broke her heart.

The couple of days she'd agreed to had stretched
to more than a week. Still, it wasn't her doing. She
hadn't detained Cedric in hospital; his own body
had. He was having a great deal of trouble
breathing.

She'd known as soon as the results from the PET
scan on his brain had come in what was wrong with
him; nevertheless, she'd run the entire battery of
diagnostic procedures, praying there'd been a mistake, praying she was wrong. She'd had one of Vancouver's leading neurologists examine Cedric and
double-check her own test results. Coward that she
was, so far Portia had avoided naming Cedric's disease for him.

Until now. She had to do it now; even though
Cedric hadn't asked, to delay any longer was cruel.

On some level, she suspected he already knew, perhaps not the label, but certainly the severity.

"'A rose by any other name would smell as sweet,'" he greeted her in his slurred voice, and she could sense the effort it cost him to sound lighthearted. To look into his eyes and smile at him was hard. She could feel tears threatening, but she fought them. She wouldn't cry in front of him; she'd already cried in private when the test results had come back.

The card she'd had delivered with the roses was prominently displayed on the bedside table, and she lifted it and pretended to read it, buying a moment to collect herself.

"'To the troubadour of St. Joe's. With love, from a secret admirer.'"

"You've got competition for my affections, Doc."

Of course the flowers didn't fool him. He knew she'd sent them, along with the fruit and the chocolates, the small radio now tuned to a classical station and the gilded hardbound copy of Rumi's verse that lay open on the bed.

"Can you sit for a while, Doc Bailey?" He motioned with his chin at the armchair beside the bed.

She sat, feeling her sorrow settle like an anvil on her shoulders. One of the benefits of working in the ER was that only rarely did she have to tell people they had a terminal disease; she'd done it, of course, but she doubted physicians ever got used to it. "We have to talk, Cedric."

He nodded and swallowed hard. "It's bad, isn't it, Doc?"

"Yes, it is." She couldn't pretend. She owed him the truth. "It's called amyotrophic lateral sclerosis, Cedric. ALS."

He tipped his head to the side and gave her a level, knowing look. "Wasn't there a ball player who had that?"

She nodded. "Lou Gehrig. It's commonly called Lou Gehrig's disease, after him."

"A famous scientist has it, too."

Again she nodded. "Stephen Hawking."

"Are there magic pills for it?"

His voice was faint and hoarse. She reached for his hand and threaded her fingers through his, as much to comfort herself as to comfort him. "No remedy that we know of as yet, Cedric. I'm so sorry, my dear friend."

"Me, too." He drew in a deep, shaky breath, and she could see that already breathing took effort. The disease was rapidly progressive, and respiratory distress was one of its symptoms—the one that would eventually end his life. She'd asked the neurologist for a prognosis. He'd said two months was a generous guess, considering how swiftly the condition had already advanced, and the fact that Cedric had likely suffered symptoms for some time.

"I knew it wasn't good."

Cedric's face twisted, and she wanted to look away from the terror in his eyes, but instead she made a conscious effort to share it.

He swallowed repeatedly, and finally managed to whisper, "It's not dying that I mind so much, Doc Portia. Living the way I do, the way I have, isn't something I'd recommend if you're looking for a fun time."

He managed a grimace that passed for a smile, and her chest ached with unshed tears. She waited for him to go on. All she could do for him at this moment was listen, and that felt so inadequate.

"It's having to be in the hospital." His weak voice wavered. "I just can't stay here, Doc. I have to get out of this place and die on my own terms. What's gonna happen to me? What's gonna give out next, besides my legs?"

His movements were stiffening, and his worsening respiratory problems meant that the medulla oblongata, the lowermost portion of the vertebrate brain continuous with the spinal cord, which controls breathing, among other functions, was involved.

As gently as she could, Portia explained the disease's probable progression. He'd be in a wheelchair before long; he'd have more difficulty breathing and swallowing.

Cedric listened. When she was done, he said, "I guess I better start looking for new digs. Place I've got isn't exactly wheelchair accessible."

Portia knew he slept in a packing box under the Georgia Street Viaduct; one of the firemen had once described it after bringing Cedric in. He'd had pneumonia that time.

"I'm checking out of here and spending as much time as I can living the way I choose." He gave her a defiant look, as if he expected an argument.

"Absolutely." She paused a moment, then added, "The hospital has a home palliative care program, Cedric."

"What's that?"

"It's a program that allows people to be cared for as long as they want to be."

He looked skeptical. "Home care wouldn't apply to me, though. I don't exactly have a house."

"I don't see why you'd have to have a house. Let me talk to the palliative care supervisor. Maybe we can work something out." Although Portia knew of the program, she didn't have all the details. She glanced at her watch. "I'll phone her right away." She got to her feet. "I have to get back to work, my friend, but I'll stop by later this afternoon when my shift is over and tell you what I found out."

She was almost out the door when he said, "I don't suppose you could help me speed up this, this...this dying thing, Doc."

Portia's gut constricted. She turned and went back to him. "I'm so sorry, Cedric. You know I can't do that."

He sighed. "Yeah, I know. No harm in asking, huh?" Again he tried to grin, and Portia's heart contracted with pity and affection.

"I'll do whatever else I can, though, to keep you comfortable. I promise you."

After leaving a message for the palliative care supervisor to contact her, Portia hurried back to the ER. The afternoon was busy, and she was grateful; of necessity, her work demanded that she put her feelings for Cedric to the back of her mind and concentrate on the immediate needs of her patients.

Her shift was almost over and she was reading the X rays of a young woman who'd broken her foot falling off a ladder, when an aide announced, "There's a man asking to see you, Doctor." She pointed to a wheelchair parked near the entrance doors. "He's waiting."

Nelson Gregory saw her looking his way and raised one hand in a salute. The other held a huge bouquet of yellow roses.

Portia had to smile. The dashing race car driver was determined, if nothing else. She had no doubt that the roses were for her and that he was about to ask her to dinner, just as he'd said he would.

She took her time with her patient, explaining to the woman exactly what bones were fractured and how long she'd be in a cast, but the whole time she was very aware of Gregory. When the woman was finally escorted to ambulatory care, Portia made her way over to him.

"Hello, Portia." He smiled up at her, his blue eyes warm and admiring. Instead of shaving off the dark growth of beard, he'd trimmed it close to his face, giving him a decidedly dangerous, piratical air. "Anybody tell you that green is your color?"

She was wearing rumpled, stained hospital scrubs. Again she had to smile at his audacity.

"Glad you appreciate high fashion. Hello, Nelson."

"You remembered my first name. I'm flattered and profoundly grateful." Then he held out the roses. "These are a small token of my appreciation for everything."

She took the roses and smelled them. Their perfume filled her nostrils. They were heavy. There must have been three dozen, wrapped in cellophane and tied with a jaunty white ribbon. They were so fresh they had droplets of dew on them. "Thank you." What was it about flowers that lifted the spirits?

"I see you've become ambulatory. Congratulations."

"I'm even being discharged tomorrow morning." His grin was jubilant. "I hear the nurses are celebrating. They say I've been a pain in the butt. How about helping *me* celebrate over dinner tomorrow evening?"

She'd all but decided to refuse, and she shook her head a little and opened her mouth to tell him no.

"Don't say no, please." There was no trace of teasing in his tone. "What's one dinner out of a lifetime, Doctor? I'll take you somewhere spectacular. I'm a gentleman. I'll do my best to be entertaining. Just give it a try, and if it doesn't work out, I promise I'll never bother you again."

"Scout's honor?" She couldn't resist gibing him a little.

"I wasn't a Boy Scout, but absolutely. Scout's honor."

The day had been stressful, and it wasn't over yet. Cedric weighed heavily on her mind and in her heart, and it had been a while since she'd had a date to look forward to. So Nelson Gregory was a playboy, so what? As he'd said, what was one dinner? He was attractive. Besides, he was in a wheelchair, with injuries that meant he couldn't exactly come on to her in any major fashion.

"Okay," she relented. "One dinner."

His blue eyes blazed with jubilation. "What's your address? Is six a good time to collect you?"

"Six is fine, but just give me the address of the restaurant and I'll meet you there."

Having him pick her up at her house felt way too intimate. She was going for friendly but impersonal.

The knowing look he gave her told her that he probably understood her reasons.

"I'll make reservations and leave a message for you with the desk clerk here in Emergency. Will that work?"

"Sure." She saw the triage nurse heading her way. "Guess I'm gonna have to get back to work now. See you tomorrow, Nelson."

"I'm looking forward to it."

And so was she, Portia realized as the rest of the day galloped past. It was all too easy to become immersed in her work and forget that she was also a woman who loved to dress up and be admired. Several times, she caught herself grinning like an idiot, wondering what Nelson's reaction would be should she arrive at some upscale restaurant wearing the green scrubs he'd admired.

INSTEAD, SHE WORE a beautifully tailored silk sheath with a matching jacket, in a color the salesclerk had called aubergine and Portia herself thought of as dusky purple.

Whatever it was, it suited her. She'd even squeezed time away from the ER to have her hair trimmed, her legs waxed, her brows shaped, making fun of herself the whole time for going to such trouble for a man she'd probably never see more than once.

As she entered the exclusive restaurant precisely at six the following evening, the startled admiration in the eyes of several male diners was mute confirmation that she looked her best.

The maître d' escorted her to a private dining alcove where Nelson was already waiting, his wheelchair on one side of the table, a chair for her on the other. His eyes, too, lit with admiration when he saw her.

"'Evening, Portia." He was elegant and shockingly handsome in a dark suit. Instead of a shirt, he had on a black turtleneck.

When the maître d' left, Nelson gazed at her for several long, silent moments, and when she was beginning to feel uncomfortable at such intense scrutiny, he said quietly, "You are so beautiful it takes my breath away."

"Flatterer. But thank you anyway." Feeling a little nervous, she looked out the window.

"I haven't been here before." The restaurant was new, but she'd heard of it—it was gaining a reputation as one of Vancouver's newest and best. "The location is marvelous…right on the water like this. And that sky…wow, just look at that sky.''

The sun was setting. The sky was on fire, the water flame-colored. A rosy glow poured down on the sailboats gliding under the Granville Street Bridge and into their night harbor.

''It's reassuring to know some things a guy arranges work out. I ordered the colors especially for you.''

''I'm impressed.''

''That's what I'm aiming for.'' His grin was mischievous.

A waiter appeared with a bottle nestled in a silver ice bucket.

''I took the liberty of ordering champagne,'' Nelson confessed as the waiter expertly popped the cork and caught the frothy overflow in a stemmed glass.

When they were alone again, Portia sipped the delicious golden wine and felt herself beginning to relax.

''Tough day at the office?'' Nelson was watching her. He silently toasted her with his glass.

''Busy, but productive. I may have found a patient I'm particularly fond of the help he needs.'' She'd met with Vanessa Thorpe just before leaving for the day. Vanessa was the palliative care supervisor, a woman in her fifties who was sympathetic to Cedric's situation.

"I have one special person who I think will take on the challenges this case represents," Vanessa had told Portia. "His name's Gordon Caldwell. He's one of my best nurses. I'll have a talk with him right away and see what we can work out."

Nelson was attentive and interested. "What's wrong with your patient?" He smiled. "He's gotta be a lucky guy if he's got you on his side."

"Actually, he's not lucky at all." Portia paused, but there was no reason not to tell Nelson. He didn't know Cedric, and she wouldn't mention his name.

"He's a street person. He lives under the Georgia Street Viaduct in a wooden packing crate. I've known him for years, and he's finally got himself straightened out, off booze and drugs. But now he's developed ALS." She described the disease, and outlined a little more of Cedric's circumstances, surprised when Nelson's face lost color.

"God, that's awful. The poor guy. Can I do anything?"

"I don't think so, thank you." Portia was amazed, both by Nelson's compassion and by his immediate offer of help. It was obvious he was affected by Cedric's plight, and she felt guilty.

She shouldn't mention her patients. Most of her dates in the past months had been with other medical personnel, who tended to view medical matters much more impartially than did civilians like Nelson.

Smarten up, Bailey. Talk about something else besides medicine, can't you?

She swallowed a mouthful of champagne for inspiration, then propped her chin on her hands and leaned toward him. "There's something very personal I have to ask *you*, Nelson." She deliberately pitched her voice low and sultry.

"What's that?" She saw a sudden wariness in his eyes, and it intrigued her. So he came across as Mr. Confidence, but he had secrets he was nervous about revealing.

It was her turn to let him stew. "I can't for the *life* of me figure out how you got those suit pants to fit over your casts," she said at last.

He tipped his head back and laughed, a deep and hearty guffaw that made her smile in response...but she also sensed his relief.

Interesting, So what are you hiding, Mr. Gregory?

"It wasn't easy," he responded. "See, I planned. My tailor came to the hospital last week. I got him to make me a couple pairs of pants that would fit over my hip brace and match some of my jackets. He put invisible zippers down the seams so I wouldn't have to wear sweatpants to take you out to dinner."

Portia let her jaw drop in amazement. "I don't believe it. Show me."

"Sure, watch." He bent over, took hold of a hidden zipper tab and unfastened the bottom of the pants a short distance. "Ta-da!" He gave her a seductive look. "Want me to go higher?"

"Tempting...but no thanks." Portia shook her head. "That's quite far enough to make my heart go pitty-pat. That zipper's brilliant. I'll bet you could make a fortune from that invention."

"I'll tell Bernardo you said so. It was his idea, not mine."

"Here's to brilliant Bernardo." She lifted her glass in a toast and drained what was left of her wine. Then she giggled. She hadn't eaten for hours and the wine was going to her head. "You know, you're the only guy I've met who actually has his own tailor. Well, no, I take that back. My mother's third husband had his own tailor, and a butler, as well." She frowned. "Or was that her fourth?"

He raised an eyebrow and refilled Portia's glass. "We're even, then, my dear. You're the only lady I've taken to dinner whose mother apparently married four separate times."

"Five. She did it again last February."

He gave a long, low whistle and shook his head. "She's either very brave or very unlucky."

"Foolhardy, I'd call it."

The waiter arrived to take their order, a complex procedure that required numerous decisions about sauces and wines. When he was gone, Nelson said, "How about you, Portia? You ever been married?"

"Nope. You?"

"Once. In my early twenties. She was my high school sweetheart, a really good person."

"So what happened?"

He shrugged and swirled his wine, not meeting Portia's eyes. "Elaine wanted a family. I wasn't ready to be a father. She remarried after our divorce—a widower with two kids—and since then they've had three of their own. She lives in Pennsylvania. Her husband teaches school there. I talk to her occasionally. She's happy and contented."

"And you? Are you happy and contented, Nelson?" It was an intimate question, too intimate for the little time they'd known each other. But Portia's curiosity had overcome politeness. The champagne had lowered her defenses, and she couldn't resist looking at his aura. Something in the colors surrounding him troubled her. It obviously troubled him, too, and she wondered if he'd tell her what it was.

His slight hesitation was almost imperceptible. "I have the kind of life I want," he finally said. "I've been extremely lucky at business. I now have the money and the time to pursue whatever hobbies attract me.''

''Such as? I *do* know you race fast cars.''

''Used to,'' he joked. ''I think it's gonna be a while before I get behind a steering wheel again. Or ski. Or sky-dive, or mountain-climb, or deep-sea-dive. And I've put my Harley in storage for the seeable future.''

The list confirmed her suspicions that Nelson spent his life looking for the next expensive and dangerous toy to play with.

''You *do* like dangerous sports,'' she said with a forced grin. ''You remind me of that old saying, if your life bores you, risk it.'' The concept went against everything she believed in as a healer, but she hid her thoughts.

Keep it light, Bailey. One date, remember? ''Is that what you're doing, Nelson? Risking your life because you're bored?''

He smiled and gave a small shrug, but again she caught a glimpse of something dark and troubled swirling in his aura.

The waiter arrived just then with their food and he didn't respond to her question. After they'd begun to eat, he said, ''How about you, Portia? What do you do for sport?''

''Yoga.''

He laughed, as she'd expected he would. "I've never tried that. Sounds kind of tame."

"You'll probably be familiar with some of the moves by the time you're done with physio," she joked, and laughed again when he grimaced.

"Besides yoga, what else? What sports do you enjoy?"

"Walking. Swimming. Biking. Dancing, I love dancing, but I haven't done it in so long I probably don't even remember how. I don't do anything that's the slightest bit dangerous. I guess I get enough of an adrenaline rush at work. A friend of mine always calls the ER docs adrenaline junkies." Portia grinned. "Joanne oughta know. She's one herself."

They talked for a few moments about Joanne, and how good she was at her job. Portia explained that Joanne had cut back on her career to raise her twins.

"Is that what you eventually want, Portia?" His tone was serious. "Marriage, kids and a career, as well?"

"I don't know," she said truthfully. "I guess every person who's single is lonely sometimes. It would be nice to have someone to go to the movies with once in a while. As for kids, I helped raise four half brothers as well as my little sister, Juliet. So babies aren't high on my priority list, at least at the moment. And Juliet still needs a lot of attention.

She's mentally challenged.'' She grimaced. "Guess all those siblings threw my biological clock out of whack.''

They ate in silence for a few moments and then he said, "How old is Juliet?''

"Twenty-four. She lives in a group home and works at a bakery over on Commercial Drive. She's very independent, but she still needs a lot of help with decisions.'' Portia waited, curious and more than a little apprehensive, to see how he'd react. She'd had dates run for their lives when she explained about Juliet.

Nelson seemed interested instead of disturbed. "Was it a birth defect?''

Portia nodded. "She's cognitively impaired. Portions of her cerebral cortex never developed.''

"I guess that's just another area that medical science can't do much about.'' There was irony in his tone. "Seems there're lots of things they have a label for but no cure.''

"They're working on it. Clinical trials are under way using drugs to improve intelligence for the severely mentally impaired. It's unlikely they'll be available in time to help Jules, but the day will come when people like her can benefit.''

"Do you find yourself wishing that time was now?''

He asked perceptive questions. Tough ones. "I

guess you can't help wishing. But Juliet has such marvelous qualities, such innocence and honesty. And such a huge capacity for love.''

He'd been listening intently. He was quiet for a moment and then he said, ''She's lucky to have you. You have a fascinating family, Portia.''

She smiled and shook her head. ''Dysfunctional, I'd call them.''

''All families are dysfunctional these days, aren't they?'' He said it lightly, and she laughed and agreed, thinking that there were varying degrees of dysfunction, and that hers was probably at the high end of the scale.

Besides divorcing every few years, her mother did psychic work for police forces around the world. Portia had grown up thinking it commonplace to have her mother converse with people no one else could see and envision horrific crimes in detail.

Nelson didn't know the half of it, and she wasn't about to tell him, she decided. Instead, she turned the conversation back to him.

''You have brothers and sisters, Nelson?''

''Nope, I was an only child. My dad's been dead for some years now. My mother lives in Florida.''

''Do you see her often?''

He shook his head. ''Not as often as I should. She's stayed very close to my ex-wife, though, and I'm grateful for that. They don't live too far apart, so they get to visit often. Elaine's kids think of her as another grandmother.''

There was a wistful quality when he spoke of his ex.

He was a strange man, Portia concluded, and, she guessed, a lonely one. He was also a man who exuded sex appeal. Portia was powerfully attracted to him. Any woman with a normal libido would be, she assured herself. Although confined to a wheelchair, Nelson Gregory had the ability to make her blood run hot.

There was also something heavy and dark and fearful that he was hiding.

CHAPTER FIVE

THEY TALKED ABOUT THEIR work after that. Nelson explained his job as a commodities broker.

Portia knew very little about the stock market, and he managed to make his explanation both informative and interesting. He wasn't a man who went on at great length about himself, however. Now he adroitly turned the conversation back to her, asking questions and listening to her answers with an intensity that was flattering, if a trifle unnerving.

He wanted to know about her medical training, and she found herself telling him anecdotes about medical school and her work in the ER, although she carefully avoided any specific mention of cases this time.

A bottle of red wine followed the champagne. They drank it leisurely as they finished the delectable meal and shared a chocolate dessert, talking now about books and movies and music. They argued and hotly defended their favorite choices. Portia loved murder mysteries; he read nonfiction. She adored romantic comedy; he preferred suspense. She enjoyed classical music; he listened to jazz.

Portia kept thinking how much fun it was to talk to him.

Outside, the sky had darkened and a row of lights blinked on along the waterfront. When the waiter came for the fourth time to refill their coffee cups, Portia glanced at her watch and admitted it was time to go, in spite of her reluctance.

"Work tomorrow, the early shift," she groaned.

"How did you get here?" Nelson asked as he settled the bill. "Did you drive or take a cab?"

"Cab. Parking is a pain down here."

"Will you allow me to take you home?" His eyes twinkled. "I'll sign a peace bond promising not to stalk you, if you let me drive you to your door."

"What a coincidence. I have one right here in my bag," she joked. "I take it on every first date, along with the pepper spray and my trusty handgun." They laughed together—Portia couldn't remember when she'd laughed as much with anyone—and then she said, "I'd love a ride home, but how are you going to manage it?"

"No problem." He pulled out a cell phone and dialed. "Okay, Charlie, we're ready to roll."

She stared at him, flabbergasted. "Don't tell me you have a chauffeur as well as a tailor?"

"Actually, I do." He appeared slightly embarrassed. "I didn't before the accident, though, so don't look at me like that. Right after the accident, I got thinking about having to special-order those taxis that cater to people in wheelchairs, and I didn't figure I could stand the inconvenience. So I bought an old limo, had it made wheelchair friendly, then hired Charlie Matousek."

The limo was waiting at the curb when they walked out of the restaurant, and it was all Portia could do to keep from bursting into laughter again when she spotted the chauffeur.

Charlie Matousek was perhaps forty, well over six feet tall, impressively muscular, with a blond brush cut, soulful dark brown eyes, a form-fitting purple velour tracksuit and a wonderful wide grin that revealed perfect teeth. And she had a little girl voice that conjured up visions of Marilyn Monroe.

"Nice ta meet ya, love," she half whispered when Nelson introduced Portia. Charlie handed her into the luxurious leather interior and then turned to Nelson.

"Just let me get you in and anchor that chair in place, honey," she murmured to him.

Nelson avoided Portia's eyes as the chauffeur expertly flipped down a ramp, rolled in the chair and positioned it in special hollows on the floor that had been designed for wheelchairs. Charlie clamped restraints on the chair so it couldn't move, brushed off the knees of her tracksuit and softly asked, "Now, where we headed?"

Portia recited her address and Charlie nodded, slamming the car door, then taking her place behind the wheel. The luxurious vehicle pulled into traffic, smooth as good wine and silent as snow. The glass partition was closed, and Portia leaned close to Nelson and whispered, "Your chauffeur calls you 'honey'?"

He blew out a breath and gave Portia an exasperated look. "She came highly recommended, and she's an excellent driver. What can I say?"

"You could try *darling,* or *sweetie pie,* or *lamb chops.*" Portia couldn't control her giggles. "Or there's always *cara mia,* or *chérie,* or *dumpling…*"

"Enough out of you, wench." He tried to appear irritated, but laughter danced in his blue eyes. "Truth is, I'm damned scared of her. She's bigger than I am. She met a couple of the guys in my pit crew this afternoon, and she had them totally intimidated within the first five minutes. Andy used some off-color language and in that *voice* of hers she told him in detail which bones she'd break if he ever swore in front of her again. She added that her father was a famous wrestler back in the days when wrestling was an honest sport, and that he taught her to take care of herself."

"I adore her." Portia was convulsed. "She's one of a kind," she gasped.

"So are you." His voice was low, and held no humor now.

Her amusement subsided and anticipation replaced it as he leaned toward her and put his arms around her. It should have been awkward with the wheelchair, but somehow he managed it with grace. He was about to kiss her, and she very much wanted to be kissed; the evening had been romantic, funny and enjoyable, and it was far too long since a handsome, sexy man had kissed her.

But the moment his lips met hers, she knew it was a mistake. The sexual tension that had simmered harmlessly between them all evening, adding spice to their conversation, became suddenly a force beyond control.

His mouth burned like fire and ice against her lips, and she recognized the sound of astonishment he made deep in his throat as the kiss deepened and grew more intense. His hand cupped the back of her head and drew her as close as the wheelchair's constraints allowed, his fingers weaving through her short hair and making her tremble as they stroked her nape and touched the sensitive spot beneath her ear.

The car stopped at a traffic light, and Portia drew

away. She was breathing unevenly, and he was, also.

"Curses on this wheelchair," he said softly, passionately. "You'll have to extend a rain check, Doc. I'd give anything right now to be able to hold you properly."

Portia didn't answer. For the rest of the short ride, she sat in silence, the music from the sound system filling in the void that had sprung up between them.

When Charlie parked the car in front of her house, Portia gathered up her shawl and her bag.

"Thank you, Nelson." Her voice didn't tremble the way she was afraid it might. "It was a wonderful evening."

"I thought so, too. We'll do it again soon."

Once more, Portia didn't reply. When Charlie opened the door, Portia got out, forcing a smile and a cheerful little wave for Nelson, another smile and a sincere thank-you for Charlie. She hurried up the walk.

Behind her she heard the motor start, but the limo didn't pull away until she'd unlocked the front door and closed it after her. She didn't turn on any lights. Instead, she watched through the window as the vehicle drove off, and then she turned and tossed her bag and shawl on the sofa, before collapsing into one of the overstuffed armchairs.

"You can't go out with him again, you know

that, Bailey," she admonished herself in the shadows that filled the room. "He's dangerous. He's sexy, and charming, and funny and quirky, and before you know it, you'll be in bed with him, casts or no casts. And then before you know it, you'll find out you're in love with him, and he's a playboy, he'll give you heart disease big-time, 'cause he's not a keeper. Remember the lady he tossed out of his room at St. Joe's. He's only in it for the thrills, and once they wear off, he'll be gone. And you'll still be here, trying to mend a broken heart."

She knew that her words were the truth. She knew that for safety's sake, she had to stay away from Nelson Gregory. But her lips still tingled from his kiss, and she smiled sadly, thinking of the laughter she and he had shared.

They meshed in some indefinable fashion. She remembered something Cedric had once quoted: *"Let me not to the marriage of true minds admit impediments."*

She wanted to see Nelson again, but it couldn't happen.

Nelson Gregory was dangerous to her health.

AS THE CAR LEFT Portia's house, Nelson said, "Charlie, do you mind if we go for a drive around the park?"

"No, sir, boss. It's a great night for a drive. Look at all those stars."

His pride had prevented him from telling Portia that Charlie was more than just his chauffeur. She was also a practical nurse, hired to help him with the physical tasks that he couldn't manage. That he needed help with things he'd never given any thought to—like getting his clothes on and off and hanging them up, getting in and out of bed, reaching things on high shelves—embarrassed him.

He'd asked the employment agency to send a man, but they'd insisted none was available. Charlie was; her last job had ended abruptly when the dear old man she was caring for had passed on, she'd told Nelson.

"What kinda music you want?"

"You choose. You want a bottle of Perrier?"

"Thanks." He leaned far enough over to reach the small fridge, extracted two bottles, tossed one up to Charlie and opened the other for himself. Settling back in his chair, he sipped it, scarcely seeing the twinkling lights of the boats on the inlet, or the span of the Lions Gate Bridge, arched like a glittering rainbow above the water.

The music Charlie chose was soft and romantic, and Nelson let his mind center on Portia...how her intellect, her humor, her physical beauty, her energy, had so delighted him. He remembered something she'd said at dinner about a patient, and over the gentle sound of the music, he asked Charlie, "You ever heard of a disease called ALS?"

"Sure have," she replied. "One of my friends who's a home-care nurse has a man with it. It's a bad one. You know somebody who's got it?"

"Portia has a patient."

"Poor person." Compassion filled her voice. "It's pretty much a death sentence—no treatment for it."

"Yeah, that's what Portia said." Nelson's throat was dry, and he swallowed two big mouthfuls of water, wondering what the hell had possessed him to mention ALS to Charlie. It was way too similar to Huntington's.

"Most of the time people die because they can't breathe or swallow," Charlie was saying. She went on talking about the physical aspects, and the problems her friend had encountered from a nursing point of view, but Nelson was no longer listening.

Instead he was comparing the two diseases. Nelson had what amounted to a specialist's knowledge of Huntington's. He should have by now; he'd studied it for years. There were definite similarities, all right. Both diseases led to a breakdown of the muscular system, and certain death. Huntington's just took longer to do the job.

When he found out that he could have a time

bomb ticking inside him, he'd divorced Elaine. It had almost killed him to do that, because he loved his wife, but he'd watched his beautiful mother grow prematurely old, her face marked with the pain of witnessing her beloved husband's painfully slow death. Nelson vowed he'd never put a woman he loved through that ordeal.

Over the years, he'd deliberately distanced himself from his mother because he didn't want her around if—when—the Huntington's began to affect him. He'd seen her with his father…feeding him, trying to communicate, going to the nursing home every single day, year in and year out, and his heart had broken for her. He'd vowed she'd never have to repeat that horror with her son.

As a commodities broker, he'd been cautious and careful before his father's illness. After his father's death, he took insane risks and paradoxically made enormous amounts of money, which brought new customers flocking. He had enough money now, invested in blue-chip stock, that he need never work again unless he wanted to. First, he'd set aside an allotted amount for the years of nursing care he would require.

Then he'd bought a motorcycle and pursued danger with a vengeance, tempting death at every hairpin turn. And that was how he'd found a way to escape the demons that haunted him. He couldn't think of anything beyond the present moment when he was riding the bike. Those times of great danger and total concentration gave him the respite that he needed to go on with the other parts of his life. And the bike had led him to other extreme sports.

Now, confined to this wheelchair, he had nothing to distract him, except perhaps the challenge Portia Bailey presented. He'd felt her withdraw after he'd kissed her tonight. Seducing her wasn't going to be easy, but the reward would be great. And figuring out how to go about it would keep his mind occupied, he reassured himself again.

"Home, boss? It's getting kinda late."

Nelson looked out the car window. He hadn't even noticed they were entering the city again, and even here, in an area usually congested with traffic, the streets were almost deserted.

The clock on the limo's console read 1:22 a.m., and he felt guilty and selfish. Charlie wouldn't complain; she was an employee, a professional, and he'd made it plain there would be no regular working hours. She'd go on driving all night should he demand it, but Nelson knew she had to be tired.

The day had been a long one for both of them; she'd come to St. Joe's that morning to pick him up; she'd helped him get settled in his apartment; she'd gotten him ready for his date with Portia.

"Home, Charlie." It would likely be another hour

at least before either of them got to bed, considering the complex routine necessary to prepare him for the simplest things. He wasn't looking forward to it, although he knew from the competent and matter-of-fact way Charlie had helped him get ready for his date tonight that he'd made a good choice in hiring her.

Tomorrow the special equipment he'd ordered would arrive—weights and bars and a treadmill for later on—and he'd begin physiotherapy with a vengeance. The promise of an explosive sexual liaison with Portia was the incentive he'd use to push himself when exhaustion threatened.

He'd call her in the morning, at the hospital. He still didn't have her private phone number, although he did have her address. Getting her home number if he wanted to wouldn't be difficult. He had contacts who'd locate it for him quickly enough.

But he wanted her to give it to him freely. He wanted to take her out again soon, maybe for lunch in the next couple of days. Did ER doctors do lunch? He didn't know, but he'd find out.

He'd send her flowers in the morning.

No, not flowers a second time. Way too predictable, too ordinary. Boring. She was an exceptional woman; she deserved something unique.

He'd think of a truly original gift, one that would make that soft mouth of hers crook into a smile, those deep-set dreamy gray eyes light up with delight.

Besides, dreaming up a surprise for her would give him something to do when he woke up sweating in the lonely small hours before dawn.

CHAPTER SIX

"COURIER ENVELOPE FOR YOU, Doc Bailey," the desk clerk announced. "It came a few minutes ago. I signed for it. You were busy with that drug overdose."

"Thanks, Jimmy." The morning had been hectic. She hadn't slept much the night before. Obviously dating when she had to work the next day wasn't a very smart move, especially when the man was Nelson Gregory. Well, it wouldn't happen again.

Now, who would be sending her something by courier, and why? Portia tore open the envelope.

Two tickets and a single sheet of folded paper fell out.

Mystified, Portia looked at the tickets first. They were for a nightclub called Flashbacks.

"Flashbacks? You ever heard of Flashbacks, Jimmy?"

"Hey, yeah, it's this vintage dance hall on the east end of Broadway, one of the best places in the city to go and shake a leg. They have live bands and a fab dance floor. It's suspended on springs or something. It's a real classy joint.'' He eyed the tickets. ''You win a contest, Doc?''

''Not that I know of.'' Portia opened the note.

For a lady who loves to dance—a rain check and a promise from a guy who plans to some-day soon waltz the night away with you in my arms. Thanks for a memorable evening. I'll be in touch long before the dancing begins—say, at lunchtime tomorrow? I'll call you.

Nelson

She reread it and felt a mixture of pleasure and irritation. Why did he have to be so damn creative? And thoughtful, as well, remembering her offhand comment about liking to dance. Why did he have to make sticking to her decision not to see him again doubly hard?

She ought to give the tickets to Jimmy, because she certainly wouldn't be using them. But she couldn't quite do it. Instead, she folded them inside the note and stuck them in the pocket of her chinos.

To not acknowledge his gift was rude, but she told herself it was the wisest move. And she'd make sure she was too busy to come to the phone should he call. He'd lose interest in her quickly enough. There was probably a whole battalion of women eager to keep him company. She ignored the tiny stab of jealousy that idea brought.

Get real, Bailey, she admonished herself. *One date doesn't make a relationship, and you know what kind of guy he is. You've obviously been without a man in your life for too long.* She vowed to accept the first invitation that came her way—as long as Nelson Gregory didn't proffer it.

BUT FOR THE NEXT FOUR DAYS, the only invitations she received *were* from him.

First, it was lunch. She politely refused.

Next came a suggestion that they share a picnic in the park. After that he proposed, of all things, attending a lecture by the Dalai Lama at the university.

Nelson was nothing if not creative, and he instinctively knew what would interest her. She felt more than a twinge of regret turning that one down. The Dalai Lama was a person she greatly admired, and she would have loved to hear him speak. She thought of going alone, but she decided against it. What if she met Nelson there? She'd feel horribly embarrassed.

The next invitation made her furious, because if anyone else in the Western world had suggested a Leonard Cohen concert at Queen Elizabeth Theatre, she'd have agreed instantly. Lenny was one of her favorite poets. But she stuck grimly to her principles.

On three consecutive days, Nelson made four appearances at the desk in the ER, asking to see her, and each time Portia had Jimmy relay the message that she was far too busy to see anyone. But each time, as well, she had to struggle with herself. Nelson was like a magnet, and it was all she could do to resist.

When her days off came, it was an enormous relief. Fortunately, they fell on a weekend. For several weeks Juliet had been hounding Portia for a sleepover. The bakery where her sister worked closed at five on Saturday, so Portia called and said she'd pick Juliet up after work. They'd spend Saturday evening and Sunday together.

Juliet was waiting on the street outside the bakery. When she saw Portia's car coming, she dropped the overnight bag she was holding and waved both arms over her head, bouncing up and down, her plump pretty face wreathed in smiles.

"Portia, I been waiting so *long*." She climbed in and wrapped her arms around Portia's neck in an exuberant hug, giving her a smacking kiss on the lips. "I love you, Portia."

"I love you, too." Portia grinned at her sister. "But don't hand me that line about waiting all day. It's only 5:05. You must have just gotten off work."

Juliet giggled. "I did just get off work. But it *seemed* like a long time. Are we going out for dinner? Can we go to that Chinese place with the smorg? Please, pretty please, Portia?"

"Your wish is my command, mademoiselle." Portia studied her sister before she pulled the car into traffic. "You got your hair cut, Jules. I like it shorter, it suits you."

"I did get my hair cut. I got it cut last Wednesday." Juliet patted her head and clasped her hands, twisting them in a figure eight against her chest and then away, a gesture that could signal either acute distress or extreme pleasure. "Stuart came with me to the hairdressing place and he watched them cut my hair. He says he likes my hair short. He says it's like petting a puppy, all nice and soft." Juliet giggled. "I really love Stuart, Portia. And he loves me back. He says it all the *time.*"

Like Juliet, Stuart Mays was mentally challenged. He'd been working at the bakery for four months, and he and Juliet were dating. Portia had met him several times, and although she was protective of Juliet, she also recognized her sister's right to an independent life and a relationship with someone she cared for. Juliet had confided some time ago that she and Stuart were having sex.

"You're taking those birth control pills, right,

Jules? And you remember what I said about you and Stuart using condoms, as well?''

"'Course I remember. I'm not stupid, you know, Portia. I'm just challenged.'' She then proceeded to repeat word for word the lecture that Portia had given her innumerable times. "It's important to use condoms because of STD's—that's sexually transmitted diseases—and I have to be responsible about sexual activity...."

"Okay, honey, okay. I'm sorry for nagging. It's just that I want you to be safe.''

"Better safe than sorry,'' Juliet stated firmly. ''That's what Mrs. Cousins always says.''

Mrs. Cousins was the housemother at Harmony House, the group home where Juliet lived, and Portia was more familiar than she wanted to be with all her aphorisms, because Juliet repeated them constantly.

"How's everybody at the house?'' Juliet was one of four residents.

"Vicky got in trouble because she told Mrs. Cousins a big lie. She said she was going to the drugstore to get sanitary supplies, but instead she went to the video place. She has this big *thing* for the guy who works there, and Mrs. Cousins found out because Louis saw Vicky and he told, and then Vicky said she forgot...she wanted a video...and Mrs. Cousins says liars have to have a good memory and honesty is the best policy, and I gotta talk to you about something really *urgent,* Portia. Okay?''

Portia was maneuvering through rush-hour traffic. ''Can it wait until later on tonight, Jules? We're almost at the restaurant now.''

''Okay, I guess so. Okay. Don't forget, though. It's *urgent.''*

''I'll remember, I promise.''

Dinner was predictable. The staff knew Portia and Juliet from numerous previous visits, and they made a fuss over them, seating them at Juliet's favorite table, a padded banquette upholstered in burgundy plush. Watching her sister laugh and joke with the waitress, witnessing her exuberant enjoyment of the simple meal, reminded Portia as it always did that Juliet's gift was her ability to be entirely in the moment, utterly absorbed by whatever was happening now.

She herself had felt that way having dinner with Nelson, Portia remembered with a pang. For that little space of time, she hadn't thought beyond the moment, and it had been restful and pleasant.

The ritual of jasmine tea and fortune cookies finally over, Portia drove home. The evening was cool, and she turned on the gas fireplace and then helped Juliet make them hot chocolate and popcorn, another favorite ritual whenever the sisters got together.

When they were settled on pillows in front of the fire, Portia said, "Okay, now tell me what's so urgent, Jules." *Urgent* was currently one of her sister's favorite words. It usually meant she was having some problem with one of the other residents at the group home.

"Me and Stuart wanna get married."

"Wow, that's a big decision." Portia had given a great deal of thought to such an eventuality. Juliet's mental capacities were limited, but her emotional needs were the same as anyone else's. Portia figured it likely that Stuart wasn't as adept at the particularities of living as was her sister—he was twenty-seven and had always lived at home with aging parents who didn't seem to expect much of him—but he likely had strengths Juliet lacked.

If the two of them wanted to marry, Portia didn't have any objections. They'd need a great deal of support, however, from the community *and* their relatives. "We'll have to talk about it, but if that's truly what you both want, then that's what you should do."

"I know it's what we should do. We really, really want to. But Stuart's mother and father won't let him," Juliet burst out. "They don't want him to get married to me," Juliet said, her voice rising and her hot chocolate spilling down the front of her pink Mickey Mouse sweatshirt as she grew more agitated. "His mother doesn't like me. She thinks I'm a bad girl 'cause I told her I like it when Stuart makes love to me."

Portia sighed. Juliet had always had difficulty figuring out what was socially acceptable as a topic of conversation and what wasn't.

"Just how did you happen to talk with Stuart's mother about liking sex with her son?"

"Well, I went there to pick Stuart up when we were going to a movie. It was *Charlie's Angels*. O-o-oh, Portia, it was so good. It's about these three women—"

"You can tell me about the movie after, Jules. What happened when you went to Stuart's house?"

Juliet frowned and took a moment to collect her thoughts. "Well, the movie place was close to his house, so I went to get him, and Mrs. Mays said Stuart had to come right home afterward and I said no, we were going to my place, and she asked was Mrs. Cousins there, and I said no, and she said Stuart couldn't come then because we shouldn't be alone and unsupervised, and I said we had to be alone to make love, and she got mad and said I was a—it was a really bad word, the *b* word."

Agitated now, Juliet got to her feet.

"And then I said I liked making love to Stuart and we're both adults over twenty-one and you said that we could make our own decisions about how we use our bodies, and I told her what you said about being responsible and using condoms, and I said I always carry them in my purse, and I showed her—I keep them in my purse all the time just like you told me to do—and then she said Stuart couldn't go out with me anymore, but he ran past her out the door and she hollered at us, and we both ran fast and then he was scared to go home—"

"Sit down, honey. You're spilling chocolate all over the place." Portia blew out a breath. "So was that when you decided to get married?"

"No, it was after that. We went to the movies and then we went to my place and then we made love and then Stuart's mother kept phoning and phoning, but I didn't answer, and then when he went home she was like real, real mad at him, and she said he couldn't see me anymore, but we work at the same place so she can't stop us, can she?"

"Okay, hon, okay. Take a deep breath. I get the picture. I just want to know the reasons for you and Stuart to get married. See, if you love each other and want to be together and know that you're right for each other, that's one thing. But if you're getting married because Stuart's afraid of his mother, that's entirely different. That's not so good."

Juliet had been sitting, but now she bolted to her feet, spilling still more chocolate. She moved around the room, waving her arms. "We're in love,

Portia. We really, really, really love each other and we want to live together in the same place and have our own television and our own bed that's big enough for both of us and then we could make love whenever we want. But Stuart's too scared to tell his mother about us getting married.''

"What does Stuart's father say about this?"

"His father only says what his mother tells him to. She's a real ball buster. Remember you told me what that was when the man said it in that movie. It doesn't really mean the girl busts—''

"Yeah, I remember.'' Portia had to smile. Her sister had a knack for using rude expressions in the right context.

"So we decided that I'll have to get pregnant. Then they'll have to let Stuart marry me.'' Juliet's voice was loud, her tone defiant.

"Pregnant?'' Portia was dumbfounded. She'd been about to take a sip of her chocolate, but she put the cup down with a thump. "Jules, hold on here. That's not a good idea at all.''

"I just knew you'd say that.'' Juliet threw herself onto the sofa and burst into loud sobs, holding a pillow over her face.

"Juliet, you know we talked about this lots of times.'' Portia got up and went over to her, rubbing her shoulders and offering tissues. "Babies are a huge responsibility.''

Juliet wouldn't be comforted. Her wails grew louder and more desperate.

"Look, it's late at night and this is something we should talk over when we're not tired," Portia finally said. "Let's run you a bubble bath. I've got some of that green stuff you like from the Body Shop. And I promise that tomorrow we'll talk more about this, okay?"

It took much promising on Portia's part, but at last Juliet agreed to put off any further discussion until the next day.

Portia ran a bath the way she had when Juliet was younger, then washed her sister's back with a soft sponge and shampooed her hair. She held a huge bath sheet ready for her when she got out of the tub.

Juliet's figure was rounded, her skin as soft as a child's. She was a pretty, sensual woman. As Portia watched her pull on her Barbie pajamas and climb into bed, she thought as she did so often how tragic it was that Juliet's body should be totally functional and her mind not.

"'Night 'night, sleep tight." Portia drew the duvet up and tucked it around Juliet.

"Don't let the bedbugs bite." Juliet yawned widely. "I love you, Portia."

Portia's eyes filled with tears. She leaned down and kissed the woman who would always be her little sister. "And I love you, Jules."

Back in the living room, Portia wearily cleaned up the chocolate mess and poured herself a glass of white wine. She turned on soft music and sank down in front of the fire, her mind troubled.

She tried to figure out what to say to Juliet the following day, what arguments might have meaning for her. There had to be a way to dissuade her from deliberately getting pregnant. If that happened, all too probably Juliet would end up a single parent. It was highly unlikely that Stuart would suddenly find enough self-confidence to move out of his parents' house.

There was also the question of whether the baby would have normal intelligence. Portia had researched this issue, and the medical consensus was that in most cases where the mother and father were mentally challenged from birth, the child might well be borderline or below. The consequences could be tragic for everyone.

And it shouldn't be entirely her problem, either, Portia mused with a surge of old resentment and anger. Juliet's father, the jerk, had abandoned all responsibility when he learned that his daughter was handicapped, but Juliet *did* have a mother who ought to be involved in situations like this.

Lydia was now living in Bermuda with her new husband. Portia decided she'd contact her mother the following morning. Juliet could tell Lydia what her plans were and hear her mother's reaction.

But Portia knew all too well that Lydia, psychically able to see and hear things invisible to the average person, was totally deaf and blind to the problems and emotional needs of her children. She professed to love Juliet and Portia and the boys, but she'd always delegated responsibility to others, nannies when her children were young, tutors and private schools as they grew older. She was hopeless at the hands-on day-to-day challenges of raising children. Fortunately, she'd always had enough money to hire others to do it for her.

In Juliet's case, Lydia had relied, from the time of her challenged daughter's birth, on Isabel, a beloved housekeeper, and on Portia.

Portia drained the wine left in her glass and turned off the gas fireplace. It was past midnight, and she'd gotten up at six. The day had been long and wearying.

Tonight was the Leonard Cohen concert, Portia remembered with a pang of regret. She wondered for a moment whether Nelson had found some willing lady to go with him. A feeling of intense loneliness came over her as she shut the lights and locked the doors before making her way upstairs to her bedroom.

It was one of those rare times when she felt sorry

for herself and regretted being single. She felt so weighed down with concern for her sister, and she dreaded the hours of patient reasoning and convincing she'd have to get through the following day. Juliet had been born with *stubborn* stamped on her forehead. Convincing her that pregnancy wasn't the answer to her problems wasn't going to be easy.

CHAPTER SEVEN

BY THE TIME BREAKFAST was over the next morning, Portia was exasperated with her sister.

"If Stuart doesn't marry you, you'll have the full responsibility for your baby, Jules," she said, trying to reason. "You couldn't stay at Harmony House. You know that babies aren't allowed. Where would you live? You'd need a baby-sitter, just for starters. Being a single parent is really tough on anyone, Jules. And you'd need extra help. It's not like having a doll, honey." She took a sip of her coffee, hoping the caffeine might give her energy for this battle, because once again, Juliet was shaking her head, her chin set in stubborn mode.

"Stuart *will* marry me. Don't keep saying he won't." She was tearing her toast into tiny bits.

"I know you believe that, but let's play worst-case scenario here for a minute. Let's pretend this is a movie and you're alone with the baby, okay?"

They'd played worst-case scenario plenty of times. It was one of Portia's most effective strategies for helping Juliet see probabilities she didn't want to examine.

"Okay. But it's only pretend, right?"

"Right." Portia's head was starting to ache. "You have a baby, you need a place to live, somebody to help with child care, and you need extra money."

Juliet looked at her from under lowered eyelids. "Our mother has lots of money. She would give me money if I asked her. We get money from those trust things already. She'd let me take more if I needed it."

Juliet was right. Money wasn't an issue. Each of her brothers and her sister, and Portia herself, had trust funds from their maternal grandparents. Portia constantly forgot about hers; she had it paid directly into an investment fund.

And if Juliet required extra money, Lydia would always supply it, Portia thought bitterly, as long as she didn't have to be involved in the day-to-day complications of Juliet's life.

"Okay, money's not a big issue. You're right about that. But Mother needs to know what's happening in your life. Let's phone her in a little while and you explain the situation to her, okay?"

Juliet started to bang the side of her head with the palm of her hand. "You tell her. You tell her.

Please, Portia. Talking to Mama makes me feel nervous.''

Most of the time talking to Lydia made Portia nervous, too, but she didn't say so. She reached out and gently restrained her sister. ''Don't hit your pretty face, honey.'' She sighed and gave in. ''Okay, you win. I'll talk to her.''

Juliet immediately calmed down, but Portia couldn't stop now. If she did, they'd be at this all day.

''So let's discuss child care and a place for you and the baby to live.''

''Okay. But it's just pretend, right?'' Juliet had abandoned the toast. Her fingers were interlaced now, her arms moving like a pendulum back and forth. She didn't meet Portia's eyes when she said in a low voice, ''Pretend we came to live with you, Portia.''

''Jules, we've discussed that lots of times before and it's not a good idea.'' Portia had to consciously cling to every last scrap of her patience. She felt on the verge of tears.

''Remember how often we talked about independence for you and for me and each of us needing privacy in our lives?'' Establishing her right to a life separate from her sister had been hard.

When she'd finished her medical training and bought this cozy house, it had taken soul-searching and a struggle with guilt, as well as a great deal of fortitude, for Portia to refuse Juliet's repeated requests to come and live here.

"Your decision to have a baby can't in any way be based on help from me, Jules," Portia declared in a firm tone. "I have a job, a life of my own." And there was that other aspect she hadn't yet mentioned. "Your baby might also be mentally challenged," she said finally, hating to mention it but realizing it was necessary. "The baby might need specially trained nurses and teachers the same as you did when you were little."

Juliet bobbed her chin up and down. "I know. Remember, you explained when you gave me birth control pills? Handicap is not a disease," she repeated in a perfect parody of Portia's lecturing voice. "But it *is* a problem, and it's best not to take chances." She reverted to her own voice. "But I know what needs to be done for mentally challenged babies. Like Mrs. Cousins always says, *been there, done that.* So I'd be the best mother for a mentally challenged baby, right?"

Portia prayed for patience.

The phone rang. Juliet was beside it.

"Portia Bailey's residence," she said loudly. Mrs. Cousins had gone to great lengths to teach her charges how to answer telephones. Juliet listened and nodded and then handed the receiver to Portia, who snatched at it, grateful for any interruption.

"Portia, it's Nelson Gregory. Don't hang up, okay?"

She closed her eyes and blew out a long breath. Today wasn't going well at all, and it was only— she glanced at her wrist—could it still be just ten-thirty in the morning? She should have an unlisted number. She'd get one immediately. Juliet, now Nelson—and on her day off!

"I'm not in the habit of hanging up on people, Nelson," she said.

"I thought maybe you'd like to go for a ride out to Steveston. It's a sunny day. I know this old-fashioned café on the waterfront where we could have lunch..."

"That's out of the question. I have company."

"Invite her along."

He was so bloody arrogant and self-assured. Why didn't he assume her company was male? Why didn't he imagine they were in bed together, enjoying a late-morning tryst? What made him think she didn't have a lover, or three or four? It probably had something to do with Juliet answering her phone.

"Thank you, but that's not possible, Nelson. Now, if you'll excuse me..." She was growing more irritated by the minute.

He sighed, a soft yet somehow determined sound

that carried clearly over the receiver. "I'm having to go to unusual lengths here, Portia. I'm convinced you enjoyed our first and only date every bit as much as I did, but for some reason you've made it difficult for me to see you again. And I very much want that. So I'm just going to sit here in front of your house until you come out and either join me for a ride or explain exactly why you won't accept my invitations."

"You're—you're sitting in front of my house?" Portia shrieked. *"Now?"* She flew to the front window. Sure enough, the long black limo was parked behind her silver Datsun.

Juliet had been listening. She came running over and peered through the window, pulling the blinds back so she could see better.

"Wowe-e-e-e, a *limo,*" she squealed. "You know someone with a *limo,* Portia? Who is it, can I go see? I love limos. Remember that time we got to go to Mama's wedding in one. I *love* limos—"

And before Portia could stop her, she raced out the door and down the walk.

Portia, barefoot and cursing under her breath, went searching for her shoes to run after her, but by the time she found them and reached the sidewalk, Charlie was out of the limo, the back door was open and Juliet was reaching inside to shake hands with Nelson as she babbled away about a disabled friend at the group home. Portia could hear bits of the conversation as she neared the car.

"And George, he has a wheelchair, too. He calls it Hiyosilver, like the Lone Ranger's horse," Juliet was saying. "What do you call your wheelchair, Nelson?"

"I've called it plenty of names, none of them polite," Nelson admitted. "But I'm really lucky, because I'm beginning to get out of it now. Not much yet, but a little."

Portia was intensely aware that he was watching her. She was also aware that although she'd showered, she hadn't bothered with a scrap of makeup. She was wearing worn jeans and an old pink sweatshirt, and the shoes she'd found were rubber thongs.

He, on the other hand, looked as if he'd just stepped out of an ad for *Esquire*, well-pressed khakis that undoubtedly had the tailor's trademark zippers installed, and a black turtleneck under a soft tartan shirt.

"Hi, Portia," Charlie said cheerfully. "Just want to tell you that this stakeout wasn't my idea. I merely take orders from the boss."

"I understand that, Charlie." Portia knew she'd greeted the woman curtly, but she was beyond annoyed and well on the way to furious.

"'Morning, Portia."

Nelson's grin would have charmed Medusa, but

Portia wasn't about to be charmed. She narrowed her eyes and pretended to glare at him. "You promised you wouldn't stalk me, remember?"

"I do. You're absolutely right, and I apologize. My only excuse is that you left me no alternative. I'm a desperate man, and desperate men do unpredictable things. Can I offer you ladies some coffee while we chat? It's latte from Starbucks." He held out a silver thermos. "And we also have an assortment of the best pastries in town, freshly baked, still warm, right here in this box." He gestured at a cardboard container.

"O-o-ooh, chocolate croissants. I'd like one, please. They're my *favorite.*" Juliet took the mug and, at Nelson's enthusiastic invitation, clambered into the limo and settled herself on the long leather seat.

"Juliet, get out of that car this minute." Portia could tell she was losing control of the scene.

Juliet, through a mouthful of croissant, mumbled, "It's okay. Honest, Portia. He's *challenged,* same as George at my house. Challenged people won't kidnap you. Honest."

"Challenged, my...my left foot. Nelson, just what the *hell* are you doing?"

His blue eyes were dancing, and he was laughing.

Suddenly, Portia's anger fizzled into nothing and she wanted to laugh, as well. This was, after all, a totally ridiculous scene, her sister wolfing down chocolate croissants in a chauffeur-driven limousine and Portia herself being pursued relentlessly by a man in a wheelchair.

"Well?" She wasn't going to give in too quickly. "I'm waiting for an explanation, Nelson."

"Looks like I'm inviting your sister to go for a ride in the country. Of course, you're welcome to come along if you wish."

"I wanna go, Portia. I *really* wanna go. Please come, too?" Juliet wasn't budging. What choice did Portia have? She swore under her breath and climbed in. "You realize this is the next thing to abduction," she snapped at Nelson. She wasn't about to let him know she was already starting to enjoy herself.

"That only happens with bad people, silly." Juliet giggled, reaching for yet another croissant. "We're grown-ups, Portia, and he isn't a bad man, but even if he was there're lots of us girls. Mrs. Cousins always tells us to chill out when we get crazy ideas in our heads. So chill out, Portia."

"All aboard and ready to roll." Charlie shut the door and got behind the wheel.

Nelson poured delicious-smelling coffee into a china mug and handed it to Portia. He filled a silver travel mug, as well, and passed it up to Charlie, along with several cream-filled pastries. He offered the box to Portia, but she shook her head. She was revved enough without a ton of carbohydrates in her system.

"You don't like croissants? I thought everyone did. You're a tough lady, Doc Bailey."

"And you're outrageous."

"You silver-tongued seductress you."

They were both grinning.

Juliet was studying the casts on Nelson's feet. "Do those come off? Did you have an operation? Did my sister put those on for you? Portia's a doctor, y'know."

Nelson explained about the accident. "These are called walking casts. In another week they'll come off and I'll get casts that I can put on and take off myself, so I can have showers and baths easier."

"That must have hurt a lot, crashing your car. I fell off my bike one time and it hurt a lot. Did it really, really hurt when you did it?"

Nelson agreed that it had.

Portia could see that although he was trying hard, he wasn't entirely at ease with Juliet. Her sister was excited, talking with food in her mouth, spraying crumbs around, bouncing up and down on the seat and, as usual, asking questions that weren't always appropriate.

Portia settled back and sipped her coffee. When Juliet was this excited, she talked nonstop. Nelson

Gregory had gotten himself into this. Now he could live with the consequences.

NELSON WAS DOING HIS BEST to hide just how ill at ease he felt with Juliet. Whenever possible, he avoided people with mental or physical handicaps. They reminded him all too vividly of his own future, and they brought back harsh memories of his once-dignified father, drooling, unable to walk, unable to make sense when he talked, unable to even go to the bathroom on his own.

But Juliet was Portia's sister, and Nelson vowed to do his best, however difficult and uncomfortable it made him feel.

Portia had challenged him, and there was nothing he appreciated more than a challenge. She'd refused his every invitation, and he'd actually begun to wonder if he would have to give up on his plan for seducing her. He'd never pursued a woman as diligently, and he'd never put as much time, energy and imagination into making himself appealing to her. Up till now, the problem hadn't been attracting women. It had been getting rid of them diplomatically when the affair was over. Sometimes even without the affair, they clung like burrs.

He thought of Corinna, the sexy blonde Lambotti had a thing for. Her actions at the party the night before the race had indirectly caused his accident,

yet Nelson hadn't so much as kissed her. Lambotti
had quit the team and disappeared after Nelson was
injured, but Corinna had sent him roses and come
to the hospital. Nelson had been in too much pain
to be tactful, and the resulting hysterical scene
wasn't one he cared to remember. He'd ended up
telling a nurse to call Security.

Having Portia in the limo with him was a vivid
reminder of how attractive she was. Her skin was
luminously clear and shining. Her eyes were that
mysterious, smoky gray that seemed to see straight
into his soul. Her short, dark hair begged to be
touched, but of course he wouldn't do anything like
that with Juliet present.

He could smell Portia's perfume, or maybe it was
her shampoo, an elusive fragrance that was tantaliz-
ing and seductive. She looked wonderful in faded,
close-fitting jeans, and he didn't think she was wearing a bra under the sweatshirt.

His body reacted strongly to her, and he winked
at her when he caught her eye, delighted when she
blushed and glanced away.

There wasn't much opportunity for them to have
a conversation; Juliet was still talking nonstop.

"Can I look inside the little fridge, Nelson?" She
was examining and admiring everything about the
limo.

"Sure you can, but better wait until we stop

somewhere. The cops could give us a ticket if they found out we'd undone our seat belts,'' Nelson explained.

"Portia used to date a cop, didn't you, Portia?''

To Nelson's delight, Juliet was oblivious to the quelling glare Portia shot her way.

"His name was Kramer,'' Juliet babbled on. "And he got some of Portia's speeding tickets canceled, didn't he, Portia? She gets lots of them because she goes too fast. And then when her and Kramer broke up she had to start paying them again, right, Portia?''

The flush came and went on Portia's cheeks. "Nelson doesn't want to hear about my speeding tickets, Juliet.'' She sounded irritated.

"Oh, but I do. I find it really interesting that you enjoy speeding. You didn't tell me that we have a love for speed in common, did you?'' He couldn't resist teasing her, and he counted on her innate sense of humor. Already he could see a reflection of his own amusement mirrored in her eyes.

Juliet was still explaining about the policeman Portia had dated for a few months. "He was a hunk. Remember you said he was a hunk, Portia?''

Portia rolled her eyes and stared out the window.

"But Kramer was way too *controlling,* wasn't he, Portia? That's why he got the old heave-ho, right,

Portia? Are you *controlling,* Nelson? 'Cause if you are, it's the old heave-ho for you, right, Portia?''

She was watching him, one eyebrow raised in mocking inquiry.

"I'd like to think not, but I suppose that's something you don't really know about yourself unless someone else tells you," he remarked.

"Oh, Portia can tell you easy. She can just look at your colors. Do it, Portia. Look at his colors and see if he's controlling.''

Nelson felt confused.

Portia was irritated. "Juliet, let's not talk about this now, okay? It's not appropriate.''

"Why not? It's very interesting, Portia. Auras are okay to talk about. You told me that once. See, Nelson, she knows when she looks at you what kinda person you are by the colors of your aura," Juliet said.

"Aura?" Nelson was mystified. "Colors? What sort of colors?''

"Juliet, Nelson is *not* interested in auras....''

But Juliet was determined to explain. "Portia sees the colors around people, like rainbows. Everybody has them. And she can tell lots of things about you just by how the colors look, can't you, Portia? She always knows if I'm getting sick or whether I'm really mad or happy or worried, even. It's called being *psychic.* Our mother's *psychic,* too, but in a different way. I'm not psychic, but I have dreams sometimes just like picture shows, where I know what's gonna happen, right, Portia? I knew that time the kitchen caught on fire that it was gonna happen. I told Mrs. Cousins, but she just said, 'Don't trouble trouble till trouble troubles you,' and then the next day the grease caught on fire just like I saw in my dream, right, Portia?''

"Juliet, Nelson is going to take us out to lunch. Why don't you tell him your favorite place and I'll bet we can go there.''

"Where would you like to go, Juliet?'' Nelson recognized the desperate note in Portia's voice. Whatever this color thing was, it was definitely not something she wanted to discuss. And the last thing he wanted to do now that he had her with him was make her wish she wasn't there. Adroitly, he led Juliet down a conversational path that had nothing whatever to do with colors. He asked her about her work at the bakery, and she gave him detailed instructions on how to load cookies on trays for baking.

IT WAS FIVE THAT EVENING by the time they dropped Juliet off at Harmony House, and Portia marveled at how quickly the hours had passed and how pleasurable they'd been.

They'd driven out to the trendy fishing village of

Steveston and walked far out on the pier. They'd eaten at a fast-food chain, Juliet's first choice, where Charlie had parked the limo in the lot and cheerfully joined them for burgers and fries and chocolate shakes. They'd stopped at a Sunday farmers' market where Nelson bought Juliet the biggest pumpkin available—Halloween was coming.

The day had turned into a long, full one, and even Juliet's homecoming took time, because after Portia and Charlie wrestled the pumpkin inside, Juliet insisted on bringing everyone in residence, including Mrs. Cousins, out to see the limo and meet Nelson. Charlie then cheerfully drove Juliet's friends around the block several times.

Mrs. Cousins had declined. "Too rich for my blood," she'd insisted with a sniff. "Doesn't do to get a taste for the finer things in life when one can't afford them."

At last, after frantic hand-waving and repeated thank-yous, Charlie drove off, and in the back of the limo, Nelson and Portia were alone, for the first moment all day. Charlie had closed the partition to give them privacy, and they looked at each other and exchanged weary smiles.

"Have you ever been around mentally handicapped people before, Nelson?" Portia slumped in the seat, feeling the usual mix of emotions after spending an extended period with her sister. Of course she was utterly drained; Juliet's frenetic energy and constant chatter were tiring, and there was always the slight anxiety of never knowing what she'd say or do next. There was guilty relief that she didn't have to cope with her sister's mood swings and stubborn attitudes on a day-to-day basis. And there was poignant sadness because her little sister hadn't developed past childhood and nothing would ever be easy for Juliet.

"Not really, no." Nelson had hesitated several moments before he'd answered. He gave Portia a wry grin. "I was scared to death at first that I'd do something stupid and wrong and hurt your feelings or hers. I hope Juliet didn't notice I was nervous."

"Not at all. She was far too excited. You were very kind and thoughtful. The pumpkin was a huge success."

He nodded. "Yeah, well, you can't really go wrong with a pumpkin, can you?" They laughed, and then Nelson was quiet for several moments.

"She's very honest, isn't she."

Portia laughed because he was so tactful. *Blunt* would have been a better word for Juliet. "Yeah, she is. It's a mixed blessing. She has no borders. She has no idea what's acceptable in conversation and what's not. So things get said that make people uncomfortable, like the stuff you really didn't want to know about her and Stuart and how she's planning to get pregnant so they can get married.'' Portia sighed and shook her head. ''That idea makes me want to lock her up somewhere until she's safely through menopause.''

She'd felt like strangling Juliet when she'd repeated to Nelson and Charlie the whole discussion she and Portia had had that morning. Portia had tried to distract her, change the subject, but when something was on Juliet's mind, it came out of her mouth.

''Sometimes there aren't any simple solutions.'' Nelson reached out and took Portia's hand in his, using his thumb to stroke the back of her hand.

She didn't pull away. She told herself the gesture was more sympathetic than romantic. But just feeling his fingers touching her skin was arousing.

''Where my sister's concerned, there usually aren't. She can be challenging, all right.'' Portia glanced out the window. They didn't seem to be heading toward her house.

''I really should go home,'' she said. ''Charlie must be sick of driving.'' She'd talked a lot to Charlie during the day; had learned that she was a practical nurse as well as Nelson's chauffeur, and that she thought he was one of the most considerate people she'd ever worked for. Charlie had a generous and easygoing way about her that Portia admired.

''I was hoping we could give her the rest of the

day off," Nelson said tentatively. "How about coming back to my condo for a drink and some dinner. We can order in—I haven't quite mastered cooking yet from this chair. And the moment you want to go home, I'll call you a cab." He gave her a pleading look. "Please, Portia? Sunday evenings are lonely."

Portia hesitated. She'd been with him for hours, but with Juliet present, they hadn't had much real conversation. It seemed silly now to go back to her earlier decision to avoid him; she'd spent the day finding out things about him. He was thoughtful and kind and generous. He didn't care one iota if people stared. He remembered exactly how she took her coffee. He laughed easily and often, at the same things that amused her. And he was dead right about Sunday evenings.

"Okay, for an hour or two. Then I really must get home."

His smile flashed, and he leaned ahead and opened the glass partition to tell Charlie what they'd decided. When he settled back, he said, "In spite of the problems, it's obvious how much you and Juliet care for each other."

Portia smiled and shrugged. "She's my sister. I'm around her more than my brothers are, but they do their best to care for her, too. We're pretty close emotionally, all six of us, although we don't see one another much.''

"I envy you your family. When I was growing up, I used to long for brothers and sisters.''

"You were an only child.'' Portia remembered his having told her so. "It must have been a lonely way to grow up. I was always glad to have siblings, particularly because our parents were never around much.''

"Juliet said something earlier that I didn't understand, about you and your mother being psychic.''

Damn and blast. Portia had hoped he'd forget that bit of information.

Why couldn't her sister keep her mouth buttoned?

CHAPTER EIGHT

THERE WAS NOTHING to do now except explain.

Portia sighed and said, "We *are* psychic. My mother's good at finding people who are lost. She touches something that belongs to someone and she can usually tell where that person is, whether he's dead or alive. She works with police departments here and in Europe, helping to locate missing people."

"I've read about investigations where they used someone who could do that. I guess I always thought it was a hoax."

"Nope, no hoax. Mom's on the level. She's helped with any number of cases that the police couldn't have solved otherwise."

"And you, Portia? Didn't Juliet say you see colored lights around everyone?" He sounded perplexed.

Portia longed to deny it, but there was no point. "Yeah, I do. I've always seen auras." Damn. She hated having to describe this. She always felt self-conscious when she did, as if she were some sort of mutation, different from the rest of humanity. "As a little kid, I just thought everyone saw them."

He looked puzzled, and she tried to explain it so he'd understand. "Everyone has an energy field that surrounds them, called an aura, visible to weirdos like me. A person's emotions and physical health determine the colors and the intensity. It's like a shimmery rainbow composed of vibrant shafts of color, and there's just a sort of knowing that's difficult to explain. I can tell where there's a major break in the light, which usually indicates injury. Or if the colors are muddy, I know there's an illness, mental or physical."

"Yeah? How come everyone doesn't see them?"

"I don't know. They've developed cameras that photograph the aura. And a great many people *do* see them, but it's not something people like me usually talk about. We get pretty tired of being laughed at." She tried to pull her hand away, but he hung on.

"Hey, don't get mad at me. I'm not laughing, Portia." His blue eyes held her gaze, intense and interested. "I'm trying to understand, is all. It's just that this whole idea of having a rainbow around me that I can't see takes a bit of getting used to. So you can tell if somebody's sick, you said?"

"Yeah, usually I can. I get a feeling about them."

She wished they'd never gotten into this conversation.

"It must make it easier to diagnose people at work. Is that why you became a doctor?"

He was relentless. Portia sighed and resigned herself to explaining as clearly as possible. Obviously, he wouldn't be satisfied with anything less.

"Sometimes it makes it harder," she admitted. "During medical training, I opted to trust the scientific method above my psychic ability, because I was making critical decisions that affected people's lives. And of course the only mention of psychic abilities was in textbooks, and was labeled as a sign of profound psychological dysfunction. If I'd alluded to being able to read auras, I'd have been shipped off to a psych ward for an assessment. But when I started practicing, I realized that for all its strengths, the scientific method doesn't always give you the whole story. So I started *looking* at people again, seeing what their colors indicated. I've relied on my ability a lot in the ER the last couple of years. But a few months ago I had a really bad experience, and I vowed never to use it again in diagnosis."

He stared at her for a moment, and she could tell the exact second that recognition dawned. "But you *did*. You used it on me, didn't you?" He sounded excited. "The day of the accident. That's how you

knew my spinal cord wasn't injured. I couldn't figure out how you could be so positive.''

Portia shrugged. ''I did that day because Joanne
asked me to. Joanne's my friend, my mentor. She's
very dear to me, I'd do anything for her. But since
then, I've tried my best not to.''

''Why not?'' He sounded astonished. ''I don't get
it. It was the best thing you could have done for me.
Why not use it on other people?''

Portia hesitated, but only for an instant. Because
of Juliet, he was already acquainted with certain intimate details of her life. It seemed natural and right
now to tell him about the mistake she'd made with
Betty Hegard, and the anguish and guilt that the
girl's death had caused her. She began slowly, but
soon the words were tumbling out.

''With Betty, I could see that she'd had an abortion,'' Portia explained. ''I could see it was causing
her terrible anxiety and guilt that in turn exacerbated
her asthma. I should have realized she was much
less emotionally stable than she appeared.''

''Isn't that tough—being able to tell when somebody's having emotional problems?''

Something in his voice told Portia that they were
talking about more than just Betty. ''Yeah, it is
tough sometimes,'' she agreed. ''But that's where
this ability to see beyond the obvious comes in. I
did pick up that Betty was disturbed, and why.

Knowing this, I should have been much more cautious in what I suggested to her.''

He was thoughtful. ''So you can actually see what's going on in somebody's head?''

''No, of course not. Not exactly.'' Explaining so another person understood was so difficult. ''What I see is a sort of gray cloud that dulls the natural brightness of their colors wherever something is wrong. In Betty's case, the color disturbance was around the abdomen and in the reproductive area.''

''So what do you see around me?'' His tone was challenging.

She'd anticipated the question. People were always curious and doubtful, needing for themselves some proof of her claims. As the car stopped and started, threading its way through busy streets, Portia allowed herself to look at him in the special way that gave her insights into things not obvious to an ordinary observer.

''Your physical injuries are healing really quickly,'' she told him. She took a breath and wondered if she should leave it at that. But he'd asked, and she felt she should tell him the truth. ''Something's worrying you, however, something that involves your head, your—'' she looked deeper ''—your brain. Not that there's any sign of disease there, just that you're worried there might be. Whatever it is, it's troubled you for a long time. I noticed it when you were brought into the ER that day, and it's still there. You can't shake it off.''

He blanched. She felt his fingers convulse on hers, and she noticed the effort he put into trying to control his shocked reaction.

"What is it you're so afraid of, Nelson?" Her tone was gentle and insistent. "Tell me. I told you my secret. Now tell me yours."

She really wanted to know. For some obscure reason, it was important to her. She had shared hers; surely she deserved to hear his.

His eyes slowly filled with tears, and he ducked his head. She tightened her grasp on his hand, trying to give him silent support. He drew a breath and then said in a flat voice, "You're absolutely right about me being troubled. See, my father died at sixty-two of Huntington's chorea." He added, "God, I can't believe I'm telling you this. It's not something I ever talk about. With anyone."

Portia swallowed hard. She was, of course, familiar with the disease, and with the prognosis. She understood instantly what his fears were, and her heart ached for him. "And you think you'll develop it, too, as you get older."

He tried for a grin, but it came out more of a grimace. "Oh, yeah, I know I will."

Her throat was dry, and she steeled herself for

what he would tell her. "You've had the test? It was positive?"

He shook his head. "Nope. What's the point of going through the agony of having it confirmed?"

She leaned toward him, took his other hand in hers and held it firmly. "You can't know that for sure unless you've had the test, Nelson. There's a fifty-fifty chance. Why shouldn't you be lucky?"

"Because my dad wasn't." His voice was harsh. "Neither were two of my uncles. Me, I'd rather wait until it happens. Waiting is hell, but knowing without a single doubt that I've got it would be even worse. I—I'm not sure I could live with the knowledge."

In some ways she agreed with him; when there was nothing medical science could do to treat a condition, a test could either set you free or make the years before the onset of the disease a living hell.

What would she do, given that awful choice? She had to admit she wasn't certain, although she thought she'd probably have to know, one way or the other.

Charlie was pulling into an underground parking area, and for the next while there was no opportunity to talk privately as they all got out of the limo and rode in the elevator up to Nelson's fifteenth-floor rooftop condo.

"Wow." Portia wandered around the spacious

living room while Charlie gathered up her things, preparing to leave. "What a great place!"

Nelson's living space was large and luxuriously masculine, furnished in dark leather softened by lavish scatterings of Aztec-patterned goose down pillows, thick rugs and bookshelves stuffed with what looked like well-used volumes. Positioned around the room were unusual sculptures and paintings, which Portia guessed weren't all reproductions. Decks opened out from sliding glass windows on two sides of the room, affording panoramic views of the North Shore and the inlet.

"Bye, Portia." Charlie waved on her way out the door. "I enjoyed meeting your sister." She touched Nelson on the shoulder. "Don't overdo it, will you, sweetie? Call me when you need me. Remember what the physio said—only a few minutes out of the chair on your feet to start with. No doing the rumba or anything. And don't be too stubborn to ask Portia for help if you need it, okay? See you in the morning." She closed the door behind her.

"Is Charlie married?" Portia was suddenly very conscious of being alone with Nelson, and she snatched at the first thing that came into her mind. He transferred adroitly from the wheelchair to a corner of the sofa, propping his casts up on a huge padded footstool before he answered.

"Nope. She's just divorced her third husband."

"*Three* husbands? She sounds a bit like my mom."

"First one died." He ticked them off on his fingers. "Second one ran off with her best friend. Third and last wouldn't work, and she got tired of supporting him so she booted him out."

"Smart lady. I guess there're any number of reasons people split up," Portia added thoughtfully.

"As many reasons as there are for them getting together in the first place. You ever been close to getting married, Portia? With someone besides that cop who canceled your speeding tickets, that is." His eyes twinkled.

She groaned. "No secrets with Juliet around." She paused a moment and then admitted, "There was one man I came close to marrying. We were both in med school at the time. It didn't work out."

"It's selfish of me, but I'm glad. Married to a doctor, you'd be out at some high-society fund-raiser tonight instead of here with a poor crip who can't even reach into that cupboard up there and get down a bottle of wine."

"I'm such a saint I'll get the wine down if you say please and tell me which bottle you want."

At his direction she found the wineglasses. She sat down beside him on the sofa and he filled them.

"To an exceptional day," he said, toasting her. He'd used a remote to turn on music, a soft and relaxing classical selection. "Now, what shall we eat? I'm starving. Those burgers were a long time ago." He opened a drawer on the table beside the couch and handed her an enormous selection of take-out menus.

She fanned them out beside her and laughed. "If I didn't know better, I'd say you were a bachelor who'd never learned to cook."

"And to think I ever doubted your psychic powers. Your choice, madam."

She studied the menus—there were at least fourteen of them. They decided on Greek—lamb kebobs and salads and roasted vegetables, then phyllo pastry for dessert.

Nelson called the order in on his cell phone, and then they sipped wine and sat in companionable silence for a time.

Portia's mind was centered on Huntington's. She deliberately scanned him, searching his aura for signs that might indicate the disease was present, if only latently. There was nothing.

"Why are you looking at me that way? Zit on my nose, something stuck in my teeth?" He gave her a quizzical smile.

"I'm trying to discern some sign that you have Huntington's," she replied. "There's absolutely nothing that I can detect."

His smile faded and she could see his vulnerability in his expression. "Would there be? If it's something I'm going to develop five or ten years from now, would you be able to tell?"

She frowned. "I'm not certain, but I think so. It would show up in your energy field. All that I can tell you is that there's absolutely no sign of it now."

"Thanks, Doc. God, talking to you helps." He reached across and gently touched her shoulder, and then, in an obvious effort to lighten the atmosphere, said, "Ever think of taking up psychiatry? A box of tissues, a couch like this one and you'd be in business."

Portia shook her head. "I'd never have the patience. That's why I love the ER. I can see the problem, treat it and not have to listen to someone's excuses for not doing what I said to do."

"Aah, a dominatrix. I've read about women like you, but I've never had the courage to really get into the S-and-M thing."

"Now's your chance." She shot him a tough look. "Wait till you see my leather jumpsuit and my whips."

They were still laughing when the buzzer sounded, announcing their food had arrived.

While they were eating, Nelson asked about the patient with ALS. Even not knowing Cedric's name, he'd remembered him.

"He's out of hospital," Portia said. "We arranged for home palliative care for him." She described Gordon Caldwell, the extraordinary nurse who was looking after for Cedric. "He's a huge man, used to be a logger. He nearly cut his leg off with a power saw, and while he was recuperating, he decided he wanted to be a nurse. He was the oldest in his class, and one of only three men, but he persevered. Now he's working in palliative care, and he's wonderful at his job. Quiet, thoughtful and just very kind and understanding. My patient really likes him, and Gordon does everything he can to help."

"How long can this guy manage on the street?"

That was on Portia's mind a lot these days. "Not too much longer, I'm afraid. He'll need a wheelchair soon, and from what Gordon tells me, there's no way my patient can go on living where he is once that happens."

Nelson nodded, his expression somber. "Poor bugger," he said softly.

Portia knew now why Cedric's plight had affected Nelson so deeply. Because ALS and Huntington's were both incurable neurological diseases, Nelson naturally identified with Cedric. "Social services will supply the wheelchair, and when the time comes, we'll have to somehow convince him that the Palliative Care Unit at the hospital is the only alternative."

Nelson didn't comment.

A short time later, when she suggested it was time for her to leave, he ordered her a cab, and only then did he take her in his arms and kiss her. In seconds, the kiss got out of control, and she wasn't certain whether she was relieved or sorry when the cabbie announced his arrival.

Reluctantly, Portia pulled away. Nelson was a complex, challenging man, and the simmering sexuality about him incited a heated response in her. She'd badly wanted to follow her body's urgings. His hands were cupping her breasts, and she yearned for them to touch her everywhere.

As she was going out the door, he said quietly, "You will go out with me again, Portia?"

Her breath was still uneven from his embrace. "Yes. I will."

"Promise?"

She looked into his eyes and saw a hint of uncertainty that touched her deeply. His vulnerability somehow pierced the barriers she'd erected around her own heart.

"I promise," she said softly, and meant it.

CHAPTER NINE

HE CALLED HER AT WORK the following Wednesday.

She was busy with a six-month-old baby who'd choked on a banana and she couldn't take the call, but she promised to return it. When the baby was breathing normally, she ordered an X ray to see if any pieces of banana were blocking the lungs. None was, and she was able to release the child to his relieved parents.

The staff lounge was deserted, so she flopped on the sofa and dialed the number Jimmy had copied down.

"Gregory here." Nelson's voice was clipped and businesslike.

"Bailey here," she responded in the same official tone.

"Portia." She could hear his relief and pleasure, and she grinned.

"Thought I wouldn't call back, huh?"

"Something like that. Being turned down so

many times before does make a guy a little insecure.''

"I promised, didn't I? You're gonna have to learn to trust me.''

"Ah, a woman of her word. How about coming grocery shopping with me when you're done there today?''

"Grocery shopping?'' Portia giggled. "You really know how to sweep a gal off her feet.'' She shook her head. "You do think of the most unusual dates, Mr. Gregory.''

"I work at it. So how about it? What time are you finished?''

"At four, but I have a date.''

"I see.'' His tone was much cooler. "Well, I guess that's that, then.''

"It is, unless you want to come along.''

There was a long pause. "On your date? Don't you think he'd mind?''

Portia was smiling to herself. She enjoyed teasing him. "Oh, no, I'm pretty sure he'd be fine with it. He's an easygoing guy.''

She'd promised Cedric she'd meet him in the hospital cafeteria for tea; he had an appointment with the neurologist at three, and she wanted to make certain Cedric kept it. She also wanted to see him away from an examining room. He was on her mind almost as much as Juliet these days.

"I must be losing my marbles." Nelson sighed. "Guys get shot for less than this. Where, and what time?"

"Hospital cafeteria, four-thirty." That would give her time to have a private chat with Cedric first.

Portia was waiting when Cedric arrived. It was distressing to see how quickly the disease was advancing; he used a walker now, and from the unsteadiness of his gait, Portia knew he'd need a wheelchair before long. She helped him get seated under the guise of giving him a welcoming hug.

Cedric had a verse for her, as usual: "'None ever was so fair as I thought you,'" he quoted, his once-powerful voice faint and flattened now. "'Not a word could I bear spoken against you.'"

The recitation brought tears to her eyes, and she hid them by going to the counter to get each of them a can of soda; she understood that Cedric would have difficulty lifting a cup. A can with a straw would be easier for him to deal with.

Back at the table, she asked, "How'd it go with the neurologist, my friend?"

"He's a nice guy, but there's not much point in going to see him again. He can't do anything to stop this, so it's a waste of time."

That was true, but it made Portia feel helpless. "What do you need, Cedric? What can we do to help you?"

He looked at her, and his sea-green eyes revealed the strain he was doing his best to conceal. "Nothing, thanks, Doc. I've got everything I need. Gordon comes by almost every day with food and stuff and I've got lots of friends. They take good care of me." His wide mouth tilted in a sardonic grin. "When they're sober, that is. But you don't need to worry about me, Doc. I'm okay."

Portia had talked to Gordon, and she knew that so far, at least, it was the truth. Cedric's friends, street people, were doing their clumsy best to help when and how they could. But they had a struggle just taking care of themselves, so the help was sporadic. Also, the nights and days were getting colder, and Cedric's ability to care for his most rudimentary needs was diminishing daily. He had to be somewhere warm, where there was a bathroom.

"Did Gordon take you on a tour of the Palliative Care Unit?" She'd arranged it earlier that day.

"Yeah, we went before my appointment."

"Do you think maybe you could stand it there?"

He shrugged and hesitated before he shook his head. "It's way too neat and clean, Doc. I need to be in my own place. I can't relax when I'm not in my own place.''

Gordon had described Cedric's place to Portia. It was a wooden packing crate lined in newspaper, furnished with an old army cot, a lawn chair, a small camp stove, a gas lantern and a few articles of clothing hanging on nails. And boxes and boxes of books, Cedric's only treasures.

"How's the fair Juliet?" Cedric obviously didn't want to talk about his own situation any longer.

"She's fine." *As long as she hasn't gotten pregnant between Sunday and now.* "She has a boyfriend. They're talking about getting married. Stuart's mentally challenged, as well. He works in the same bakery as Juliet.''

"Is that so." Cedric smiled. "Good for them. Tell her from me I wish them well. Never got married myself, but I hear it's very companionable.''

"I'll pass your good wishes on." Portia could tell he enjoyed having her confide in him about her personal life, and she was about to mention that a friend would be joining them when she caught sight of Nelson's wheelchair coming through the cafeteria door.

"I hope you don't mind, Cedric. I asked a friend to join us. He's the guy in the wheelchair by the door.''

Cedric turned and looked, and at that moment, Portia realized she'd made a huge mistake. Nelson was a handsome man, and in spite of the wheelchair, he gave the impression of being fit and healthy, everything Cedric wasn't. She realized something else, too—the depth of Cedric's feelings for her. His eyes let show that he was in love with her. And he was jealous.

NELSON ROLLED UP to the table and Portia introduced the two men. If Nelson was shocked by Cedric's appearance, he hid it well. He held his hand out and shook Cedric's.

"Pleased to meet you," he said as if he meant it.

Cedric didn't reply, and the awkward silence lengthened.

Nelson said, "I'm gonna grab a coffee. Can I get you two more soda? Maybe tea or something?"

Both Portia and Cedric declined.

Nelson made his way to the beverage dispensary and filled a cup with coffee.

Portia reached across and took Cedric's hand in hers. It was no use pretending nothing was wrong. "Cedric, I'm so sorry. I thought you two might enjoy meeting each other. It was stupid of me."

Cedric drew a ragged breath, and Portia could see him struggling with his feelings. "It's me who's stupid, Doc Bailey,'' he said with a failed attempt at a smile. "I guess I like to pretend I'm your only admirer.''

She hadn't time to respond before Nelson came back. He was balancing a cup of coffee with one hand and propelling his chair with the other, and the chair bumped against the table leg. Hot coffee sloshed on his hand and he jerked, spilling the rest on Cedric's arm.

Cedric yelped and Nelson swore.

"Damn, I'm sorry." Nelson grabbed a handful of napkins. "God, that's hot. I'm so sorry."

Portia rushed over to the ice machine and came back with two soup bowls filled with crushed ice. "Put this on it," she instructed.

Nelson, obviously embarrassed, did as she said, and so did Cedric. "Lucky I didn't get you, too, Portia," he growled. "I can't believe how clumsy I am in this bloody chair. There ought be a warning sign on my forehead that says Approach At Your Peril.''

It wasn't a bad idea, Portia thought. But not for the reasons Nelson meant.

The burns were minor, and once she'd finished examining them, Portia could see Cedric had relaxed a little. The accident had somehow dissolved his antagonism. "Maybe you oughta write down some ground rules for me about wheelchairs,'' he said to Nelson. "I'm gonna be using one soon. It would help to know what I'm up against.''

Nelson nodded. "There should be an instruction book for the bloody things. I think the worst is being invisible. For some reason a lot of people don't acknowledge you when you're in a wheelchair. You're too close to the ground. They not only ignore you they trip over you.''

"So what happened to you?'' Cedric gestured at the casts, and Nelson explained about the race car accident.

"What caused it?'' Cedric wanted to know.

Nelson hesitated, and then he said, "It was my fault. I didn't think so at first, but now I do. I was reckless.''

Cedric was fascinated. "I've never met a race car driver. I always wondered how going that fast would feel.''

"It's a real high, but racing can suck you in and then spit you out long before you're ready to quit,'' Nelson said. "You're at war not only with your car, but also with the forces of nature. Plus it's tough to remain a nice guy and still do what it takes to win, because you've got to be pushy and self-promoting just to stay in the game.''

"Sounds like life," Cedric remarked. "How long you been in it?"

Nelson gave a quick rundown on his career as a race car driver, and Portia listened, fascinated. She'd never really asked Nelson about racing. She hadn't known that he owned the car he'd driven, or that any car could cost as much as it had.

Cedric was hanging on his every word. "Think you'll get back into it?"

Portia hadn't asked that, either. She'd assumed no one in his right mind would climb back into a race car after sustaining the injuries and coming as close to death as Nelson had.

"I'm not sure. Right now all I can think about is being able to walk again and drive an ordinary car."

"I'd give a lot to be able to drive a car again myself. I haven't for years, and I guess I waited too long," Cedric said matter-of-factly.

Nelson gestured at the walker. "At least you're on your feet."

"Not for long. I've got ALS."

Portia held her breath. Would Cedric feel uncomfortable discussing his condition with Nelson? Would Nelson reveal that she'd breached patient confidence and told him about Cedric, even though she hadn't mentioned names?

Cedric gave Nelson a quick and textbook-accurate description of the disease.

Nelson held his gaze steady on Cedric and nodded when he was done, just as if Portia had never said a word. "My father had something similar," Nelson said quietly. "Neurological disease is one hell of a thing."

Cedric nodded, and Portia was aware that an invisible bond formed between the two men when Nelson mentioned his father.

"Here's Gordon. He's gonna give me a lift home," Cedric said as the tall, husky nurse came toward them. Cedric introduced Nelson and Gordon, adding that Nelson had driven in the Indy. Cedric was obviously enjoying himself, and Gordon was suitably impressed.

The men talked for several moments about some technicalities of motors that Portia didn't begin to understand, and then Nelson said, "If either of you ever wants a ride in my car, let me know. It's been repaired, and although I can't take you for a spin myself at the moment, one of my pit crew would be happy to." He jotted down his phone number on a napkin and handed it to Cedric, who looked happier and more excited than Portia had seen him look since his diagnosis.

When they were gone, Nelson slumped back in his chair and closed his eyes for a long moment.

"You okay?" Portia reached across and touched his scalded hand. "Maybe I should get you something for that."

He opened his eyes and she could tell by the way he glanced at his hand that he'd totally forgotten about the burn.

"You're full of surprises, Portia." He didn't sound critical, however.

"You guessed, of course, that Cedric is the patient I told you about. He's also my dear friend," she said.

"I can see why. He's not at all what I imagined a street person to be. How long has he got?"

Portia sighed. "Nobody knows that for sure except God. I'd say not long at all. His disease is progressing at a rapid rate."

Nelson nodded. "And he still lives on the street?"

"Yeah. He has some kind of shelter, under the west end of the Georgia Street Viaduct. Gordon says there're steam pipes that provide a little heat."

"If I found him a decent place to stay, no strings, would he accept?"

"Nope." The offer touched her heart. "But that's very sweet of you." She explained about the hospice. "There's room for him right now, but he won't hear of it. I'd say he might get Gordon to call you about the race car thing, though. He was really intrigued by that."

"I hope he does." He eyed her for several moments, that silent appraisal she'd become accustomed to with him. "You look radiant. How can you do what you do all day, deal with patients like Cedric, and still look radiant at the end of your shift?"

"Cosmetics," she said, lowering her voice as if her disclosure were a guarded secret. "You just slather on this miracle cream and voilà! Instant radiance." She hadn't used anything all day except soap and water, an eyelash curler and some lipstick, but he didn't have to know that.

"Remind me to buy stock in the company."

She smiled, but something he'd mentioned earlier was on her mind. "Nelson, what did you mean when you said the accident was your fault, but you didn't think so at first?"

He shrugged, and for a second she thought he wasn't going to answer. Then he said, "There was a misunderstanding with my head mechanic, a guy named Lambotti. He figured I was after his woman. I thought he sabotaged the car to get back at me."

"And were you?" Portia raised a quizzical eyebrow, trying to appear only mildly interested. "After his woman?"

"Hell, no. It was the other way around, but he wouldn't believe that."

"Have you talked to him about it?"

Nelson shook his head. "He disappeared right after the crash. Nobody's seen him since."

She clamped her mouth shut. She wasn't about to ask the next question, even though it was obvious.

He guessed, though, and grinned at her. "Yup, I saw the lady. She came to the hospital bearing flowers. I was too sick to be tactful. I had the nurses call Security and boot her out."

"Ah. I heard about that."

"How come you never asked me about it? You must have figured I was some kind of arrogant playboy, evicting women from my room."

"I did at first. But relax. Now I don't." It wasn't entirely true, though. She still wondered what would happen when his injuries healed. Would he go straight back to the kind of life he'd led before the accident?

He grinned at her and shook his head. "You're one of a kind. Ready to go grocery shopping, Doc?"

It wasn't the time to bring up the future. "Absolutely."

"My chariot awaits. Charlie's visiting some old

pal in the X ray department. I'll just give her a buzz." He dialed his cell phone, and minutes later they were in the limo, with Charlie at the wheel.

They headed for Yaletown, and Charlie parked. "I love it here. There's a discount clothing store just down the block that has sexy stuff in my size," Charlie said, hurrying off. "Call me when you're ready. Just take your time."

Portia and Nelson made their way toward an open-area marketplace called Urban Fare.

"Been here before?" Nelson asked as they went inside. The place was crowded with well-dressed yuppie shoppers, and the noise level was in the high-decibel range. Kiosks lined the huge open space, and there were long lineups at the cash registers.

"Nope. I've heard of it, but I've never had a chance to explore much down here. Doctors don't get out and around. We tend to eat and sleep and work. Boring as hell. But I thought you didn't cook."

"After the way you lectured me about the dangers of living on restaurant food, I decided to turn over a new leaf," Nelson said.

Portia had to bend over and put her ear close to his mouth to hear him.

"Now, what shall we have for dinner, Doc?"

He hadn't mentioned taking her to dinner, but the smells were already making her hungry and reminding her that she'd missed lunch. She gazed around, amazed and impressed at the variety and beauty of the food on display.

"I wouldn't exactly call this a grocery store, Nelson. It's more like major take-out gourmet heaven."

Delis lined entire aisles, selling mouthwatering prepared selections of every kind of food imaginable—lasagna, moussaka, meat and vegetable pies, salads so artistically prepared they looked like art exhibits, pizzas, grilled vegetables, pastries, cakes, breads, glass cases containing exotic desserts.

Portia and Nelson decided on a round loaf of oatmeal bread, a country-style lamb stew with dumplings, endive salad and apple torte. Nelson also bought lasagna, peasant pie, borscht and baked vegetables, all ready for freezing.

"There's nothing like a home-cooked meal," he said, his wheelchair loaded down with boxes and bags and foam containers. They finished off with a bag of wonderful-smelling coffee beans and a quart of homemade vanilla ice cream.

"How would you feel about driving the limo home? That way we can let Charlie shop to her heart's content."

"I've never driven a limo, but I'd love to give it

a try," Portia said. "As long as you're fully insured."

"Totally," Nelson assured her with a grin.

"Okay. And you have my permission to back-seat-drive. Although considering how you got yourself in that wheelchair, maybe I'd better rely on my own instincts."

Nelson called Charlie on his cell phone and told her they wouldn't need her, and with much laughter and a few near calamities when some of the food almost slipped off his lap, they managed to get Nelson's chair and the groceries loaded.

Portia climbed in and started the motor, then pulled cautiously into traffic. She was nervous for the first few moments, but she soon adjusted to the size of the luxurious vehicle, and by the time they'd reached Nelson's condo, she was enjoying her role as chauffeur.

Once they had everything in the condo, Nelson helped Portia stow it away. They slid the stew into the oven, and together they set the table.

"You have beautiful dinnerware and cutlery," Portia remarked as she set the dark brown heavy plates on bright yellow mats and arranged the simple but elegant knives and forks beside them. "Everything matches. I can see I'll have to do some updating if you ever come to my place for dinner.

I use dishes Juliet found for me at a garage sale and gave me for Christmas. They're yellow and green with a border of roses.''

"I don't know the first thing about dishes or cutlery. When I bought the condo I hired a decorator. She chose everything.''

Portia folded the brown linen napkins and he put them into heavy wooden holders. She lit squat beeswax candles and placed them in the middle of the table, and he dimmed the lights and turned on a selection of jazz CDs.

"The room's so perfect it looks like a setup shot for a TV commercial,'' she commented. *Or the ideal setting for an intimate dinner leading to a seduction.* She remembered the hungry kisses they'd shared and a shiver ran down her spine. Given the raw sexual attraction between them, seduction would be a mutual endeavor when it happened— and somewhere deep down Portia accepted the fact that it was inevitable. Being near him made the hairs on her neck stand up.

The timer dinged. "Dinner's ready.'' She brought in the stew and the bread while he managed the salad.

He held her chair for her, leaning from his own to perform the courtly gesture, and she liked it. They ate with honest hunger for a few moments.

"This bread is wonderful. We had a cook once when I was a kid who made us homemade bread like this." Portia buttered a second slice and mopped up gravy with it.

"Tell me what mealtimes were like when you were a little girl."

"They could get pretty wild when the boys were around, but usually they were off at boarding school. Often there'd be just Juliet and me for dinner. We always ate in the kitchen. My mother and whatever husband she had at the moment weren't around much. They traveled and left us kids in the care of household staff. Because we moved so much, the staff changed a lot, but we had one housekeeper named Isabel who moved with us for a number of years." Portia shook her head. "Good old Isabel, she stuck with Mother through husband after husband and move after move. Juliet and I adored her."

"Where is she now?" Nelson was paying close attention to her every word.

"She died five years ago. I thought Juliet would never get over it. She went into a depression for months. She was living at that time with my mother in San Diego. When Isabel died, Mother moved Juliet back to Vancouver so she'd be closer to me. I found her the placement at Harmony House. Without Isabel around, Mother couldn't cope with Jules."

"You told me your mother's now living in Bermuda."

Portia nodded. "Just outside of St. George's. She and Malcolm Pritchard, her latest husband. They travel a lot. Mother can't stay in one place very long."

"So you have full responsibility for Juliet."

They were finished their meal, and Portia got up and took the plates to the sink.

"Yup," she said as she served their apple torte and plopped ice cream on top. "She loves her, but she's at a loss when it comes to coping with her. And Juliet says Mother makes her nervous."

He rolled his chair over and dealt with the coffee machine. They were seated again, devouring the crunchy sweet dessert when he said, "Where are your brothers?"

"Conrad and Richard are the youngest. They went off to Australia last year to work on a sheep ranch. They finished their schooling in England. The other two are businessmen. Henry's in Alaska. Antony's in Los Angeles. Henry runs a small airline that transports freight. Antony's in the restaurant business."

"Do you see them much?"

Portia shook her head. "Henry got married two years ago. We were all at the wedding, but that's the last time we were together. We talk on the phone a lot. We're close, but we don't see one another much. Except for Juliet and me, that is."

"Any new developments with her and Stuart since Sunday?"

"God, I hope not." Portia shuddered and then groaned, "How am I going to get it through her head that pregnancy isn't the route to happily-ever-after?"

He hesitated for a few moments. "Would it help any if I spoke to her?"

Portia shot him an amazed look. Most people would run a marathon with a broken leg before they'd offer to get involved in Juliet's difficulties. "That's really generous of you, but I'm not sure it would help. I'm going to talk to her again on my days off. Hopefully I can get her to see reason."

"If there's anything I can do, just say the word."

"Thank you." Her words were heartfelt, because his offer made Portia feel that she wasn't alone with her sister's problems. To know that he meant what he said was comforting.

They had coffee in the living room, side by side on the leather sofa. Portia noticed that Nelson was already much more adept at transferring from his wheelchair; he was also beginning to put weight on his injured feet. She commented on it.

"I have a fully equipped gym just off my bedroom. I added a few things the physio recommended and I've been working out hard the past couple days," he admitted. "I'm gonna get mobile again as fast as it's humanly possible."

"Then what?" She pulled her legs up under her and sipped her coffee, aware that his shoulder was only inches away. "Back to race cars and life in the fast-and-dangerous zone?" Her voice had an edge.

"Does that bother you, Portia?"

"Yeah. I guess it does. I hate to think of you risking your life just for the hell of it."

He didn't answer. She turned and looked at him, and the intense expression in his blue eyes made her breath catch. He silently took her cup from her and placed it on the coffee table, then he reached out and drew her into his arms. As he held her against his chest, she could hear his heart hammering.

"That's not why I'm working my ass off, Portia. I have to get fit again so I can make love to you the way I want to," he murmured, his voice deep and seductive. "Not being able to pick you up and carry you into my bedroom is torture."

"You've seen *Gone With the Wind* one too many times," she chided, but her voice had a catch. If thinking about making love with him was erotically arousing, having him talk about it was doubly so. She asked herself if she knew what she was doing— or about to do—and assured herself she didn't.

"I have two working legs of my own," she told him. "I can walk to your bedroom by myself." She took a shaky breath. "Unless your hip...unless you can't...?"

He didn't answer in words. Instead, he kissed her, a kiss so filled with hunger it sent a shudder through her. "Walk," he pleaded. "Please, walk down the hall and turn left at the end. I'll be right behind you."

PORTIA DID AS HE ASKED, not looking back to watch him get into his chair or see him wheeling after her.

The hallway was softly lit. The door at the end was ajar, the room large. She went in, dimly aware of dark, smoky-blue walls, a skylight, an immense bed with a navy-checked duvet and snowy pillows. A device to help him transfer from bed to chair had been installed in the ceiling. As she crossed the room, music began to play softly from hidden speakers, an Italian tenor with a voice that touched her heart.

Nelson was replacing the music remote on a small

cabinet, removing something from one of the drawers, and when he turned, he looked at her.

She held his gaze as she slowly unbuttoned the shirt she was wearing and slid it from her shoulders. Her bra was the soft cotton sports type she preferred for work. She heard his breath catch as she pulled it off.

He wheeled across the carpeting and smoothly hoisted himself onto the bed, then lifted the sweater he was wearing over his head. Dark curls covered his broad chest. Then he guided her down on the bed beside him, reaching out to cup her breasts in his palms. He made appreciative noises as he took each nipple in his mouth, and heat and need streaked through her.

"You're breathtakingly beautiful, Portia." His voice was husky.

"You're not exactly repulsive, Nelson." She deliberately kept her tone light. *Keep it simple, Bailey. This is a delightful game we're about to play. Just remember that's all it is—a game.*

He kissed her, taking his time, exploring her mouth and her throat, and she could feel the control he was exerting in the tremor of his fingers as they stroked every inch of her. She rubbed her breasts against him, loving the sensation of soft chest hair against her tender skin.

Her fingers found his erection, which was straining against his trousers. He stiffened when she touched him and groaned. He loosened the belt buckle at his waist to make it simpler for her.

She caressed him, learning the size and shape and weight of him, loving the intense heat he radiated, the little choked noises he made as she became bolder.

"Let me help." He sat up for a moment and undid the hidden zips that allowed the pants to come off.

"I might have guessed you'd be the sort to wear black underwear," she said, struggling to keep her voice under control. "Sexy man." She slowly drew the briefs down his legs.

"Not as sexy as this," he replied unsteadily, undoing her khaki pants and running a finger under the elastic of her white cotton bikinis. The sensation of his rough finger against her abdomen made her shudder. She shinnied out of her slacks, taking off her panties at the same time, aware that her breath was coming as if she'd been running. Her skin felt as though it was burning.

God, she wanted him. She wanted him *now*.

He edged his hand between her legs, and his touch came close to putting her over the edge. "You're so wet."

"I want you in me." Urgency had become desperation. "Please, Nelson. How can we do this without hurting your hip?"

"Like this, love. Like this." He gripped her waist and half lifted her over him, and she was dimly aware of how strong he was. As her legs parted, she realized he was rolling a condom into place. Then he slid inside her and the sensation was overwhelming. She moved on him, feeling the tremors begin deep inside, and then she soared as her body clutched and claimed him and pleasure took her over the top.

"Open your eyes, love."

When she did, she found him gazing at her, his blue eyes like lasers. "I need to look at you. I need you to watch me," he whispered. And then he bucked beneath her, his face contorted with a reflection of the delight she'd felt a moment before.

Once the spasms ended, Portia sprawled across him, breathing in the musky odor of his skin, floating in the hazy aftermath of exquisite pleasure.

"I'm not sure this is the best thing for your hip," she murmured. "Are you certain I'm not hurting you?"

"Absolutely not." He dealt with the condom, and then closed his arms around her to draw her back against his chest. "Lie on top of me, just for another few moments."

She did, every muscle relaxed. "It was so good," she mumbled, already on the verge of sleep.

"We haven't come to better and best yet, but I promise you we will."

She smiled. "Can I have that in writing?"

"Certainly." He was stroking her back, his strong hands soothing on her skin. "I've dreamed of this from the moment I first saw you."

"Now, that's an exaggeration," she said with a smile. "I doubt that sex was uppermost in your mind when I walked into the ER that day."

"Well, maybe the second time I saw you," he amended, and she knew a lazy grin accompanied the words. "You're the sexiest doc I've ever laid eyes on. I'm surprised you don't have your own fan club over at St. Joe's."

"I do. Cedric's my fan club." She closed her eyes. "I'll move in a minute."

But his slow hands on her back were hypnotic, and she drifted off, instead.

NELSON WENT ON STROKING HER, even though he could tell by her breathing she was asleep. His hip was on fire and before long he'd have to move to ease the pain, but for the moment the pleasure of having her slender body spread-eagled over him, warm and soft and fragrant in his arms, outweighed the need to ease his position.

When she awakened, she'd probably insist on going home; she'd mentioned having to be at work early the following morning. He wanted to keep her with him as long as possible.

Loving her had been everything he'd dreamed. Passionate and uninhibited, she'd responded to his every touch, however limited his injuries had kept him.

These moments after sex were special because of the euphoria they brought. Every worry eased; every muscle relaxed. For these few moments, he didn't feel alone, and the weight of the future seemed lighter.

He thought about their next date. There was a stage performance of *Les Misérables* coming. He'd find out when her days off fell and get tickets. So far he hadn't really taken her anywhere special; the things they'd done had been very ordinary. Still, he couldn't remember when he'd had such fun just being with a woman. Most of the women he'd dated before his injury had been high-maintenance, expecting to be wined and dined and entertained in a manner now impossible for him.

Portia, on the other hand, seemed content with the limited scenarios.

More than content. She'd seemed pleased just to be with him. Gratification stole over him. She was delightful to be with.

He thought about her strange ability to see things invisible to the rest of the world. There was no question in his mind that she could do exactly what she claimed; all the proof he'd needed was that moment in the ER when she'd looked into his eyes and assured him he had no spinal damage.

And she'd told him that for now, at least, there was no trace of Huntington's. If only he could trust her instincts completely.

He felt her stir, and relished her short silky hair against his cheek, the regular thrumming of her heart against his chest. If things were different, if no sword of Damocles was hanging over his head, she was a woman he could come to love.

The thought flickered across his mind, and as quickly as it had appeared, he squashed it. The kind of long-lasting love men and women shared wasn't for him. He only had to remember what love like that had done to his mother…how old she'd grown, how fragile and sad, as they waited for his father to die.

He'd vowed long ago that he wouldn't put any

woman through such an ordeal, and he hadn't changed his mind.

For this one small moment, though, he could love Portia, as long as he kept in mind that it was temporary, that the time would come when he'd have to end it.

But not yet, he assured himself. Not yet. They were only at the beginning. He didn't have to think of endings yet. He ran a hand lightly down her spine, enjoying the march of vertebrae, the dip of her waist, the delicate roundness of her buttocks.

And he felt himself growing hard again, wanting her with a ferocity that surprised him. Her body was open to him, and if he moved just a little, he'd slide into her heat.

CHAPTER TEN

HE QUICKLY TOOK CARE of the condom situation, and was already making love to her when she awoke. She lifted her head and he kissed her, his tongue signaling urgency.

But this time the journey was longer. He stopped her frenzied movements with a firm hand on her buttocks, forcing her to slow down, mercilessly building the suspense, leading her higher and higher with him, until the tension and anticipation were all but unbearable.

When the ending came, she heard herself calling, felt herself falling, knew his strong arms were holding her safe even as she burst apart and re-formed, sated. His cry echoed hers, and she couldn't have told where his body ended and hers began.

This time she rolled off him. ''We're gonna reinjure your hip, and explaining how it happened isn't something I want to get into with any of my colleagues,'' she panted.

''Y'know, I think we're getting better at this. It

just takes lots of practice." His tone was thoughtful, and she giggled. Then she glanced at the bedside clock and gave a yelp. "I've gotta go. I'll never make it up in the morning."

"Aren't you hungry? I am." He retrieved a pair of soft cotton drawstring pants from under the pillow and pulled them on. "I'll make us some grilled cheese sandwiches. With dill pickles. And I've got some frozen fries. What d'ya say?"

She should go, she knew it. But she *was* hungry.

"Okay. Shall I use that bathroom I saw down the hall?" She guessed that the ensuite would be more convenient for him to use with his chair.

"Meet you in five."

It was more like fifteen by the time Portia had showered and got her clothes on.

Nelson was already in the kitchen, an electric frying pan plugged in. He'd set it on a chair so he could reach it easily, and he was buttering slices of bread on an overturned cookie sheet on his lap.

He handed her the block of cheese and a grater.

"Grate this. I'll chop up some onion and slice the tomatoes. I'll have you know these aren't your everyday grilled sandwiches. These are *cordon bleu.*"

Within minutes, they had the sandwiches assembled. He plopped butter in the pan, and soon the smell of melting cheese and frying bread filled the kitchen with a mouthwatering aroma.

"You've been misleading me. You *can* make things from scratch." Portia was leaning against the counter, munching on a garlicky dill from the jar he'd taken from the refrigerator. There was a feeling of cozy companionship in the room.

"Sorry to disappoint, but grilled cheese is my entire repertoire. I learned to make them out of desperation when I OD'd on Chinese takeout one time. How about you, Portia? You cook?"

She rolled her eyes and shook her head. "Not anywhere near. Think basic, so basic it's probably not even called cooking. Boiled macaroni, say, with a tin of tomatoes and some frozen peas dumped in, or stir-fry." She tipped her head to the side and considered. "Actually, I *do* make good stir-fry. I'll do one for you some day soon."

"I'd like that." He flipped the sandwiches. "There's cola in the fridge. You have to drink cola with grilled cheese. It says so in my French cookbook."

"Right, boss." She got them each a bottle, and by that time the sandwiches were ready. He slid the fries out of the oven, brown and crisp. They ate at the round kitchen table, with paper towels for napkins.

"See, the service in this place goes downhill fast," he said. "We start out with linen and silver, and here we are only a few hours later with all the trappings of a soup kitchen."

"Looks like now that I've given you my body, you've stopped trying to impress me," Portia sighed. "I might have known I'd get no respect in the morning."

Instead of laughing as she'd expected he would, Nelson laid his sandwich down and reached across the table to take her hand in his and gaze into her eyes.

"I don't want to impress you, Portia. I want to surprise and delight you. I want to hear you laugh. I want to make love to you every way there is and in a few ways I intend to invent. I want to spend time with you. Talk. Do things like this. I want to share whatever's going on in your life." He gestured at the sandwiches and lowered his voice. "Tonight's been special for me. I hope you feel the same way."

She blamed exhaustion for the tears that suddenly burned at the back of her eyes. She didn't want him to see them, so she took another bite of her sandwich and searched for words to lighten the atmosphere, but the naked honesty in his voice and in his expression made it impossible. She settled for the truth.

"I feel exactly the same way, but now I really *do* have to go home. Some of us have to work in the morning."

"Finish your sandwich. I'll call a cab." He dialed, and when the buzzer sounded downstairs, announcing the taxi's arrival, he drew her gently down to his level and kissed her.

"Sleep well, my darling."

She loved how he said *darling*. "I shall, although it'll be awfully short." Portia hurried out the door.

When the cab pulled up at her house and she tried to pay, the driver shook his head. "It's taken care of. Mr. Gregory has an account with us."

Nelson was a chivalrous, thoughtful man. She liked that about him, as well as a dozen other things, like his thoroughness in bed and the intensity he brought to making love. She *really* liked that.

Be careful, Bailey. He's a rich playboy, and chances are he's fickle.

Well, she'd been known to be fickle herself, she mused as she ran up the walk and unlocked her front door. Inside the house, the light was blinking on her answering machine. She smiled and pressed the button, half expecting it to be Nelson bidding her a final good-night.

"It's your sister, Juliet Bailey," her sister's loud, plaintive voice announced. "Where are you, Portia? I really need to talk to you, okay? It's *urgent*. So call me back right away when you get home, okay?"

Damn. She'd phone Juliet first thing in the morning. She'd planned to find time this week to have another talk with her, but she hadn't. As she stripped off her clothes and tumbled into bed, niggling apprehension about Juliet vied with vivid memories of making love with Nelson, but exhaustion soon overcame thought, and she fell asleep.

Portia overslept Friday morning, leaving her barely enough minutes for a fast shower before she raced off to work. The day was frantic; two major pileups on the 401 and an explosion in a paint factory meant that there was no time to use the bathroom, much less call Juliet, who'd left two messages with Jimmy during the day.

By the time her shift ended, Portia had forgotten she even had a sister. She felt the way she used to as an intern after back-to-back double shifts: thickheaded, irritable, headachy and drained of every concern except finding the nearest horizontal surface and sleeping as long as possible.

She staggered out of Emerg, climbed into her car and drove home. It was only when she saw the blinking light on the answering machine that she remembered Juliet.

With a groan, she dialed her sister's number.

"Where have you been?" Juliet was angry. "I called and called. I even used your cell phone. You always tell me I can get you anytime on your cell, but a lady kept saying this customer is not available, and she wouldn't answer me when I talked."

Portia needed aspirin. "I'm so sorry, Jules. It was crazy at work. I guess I had my phone turned off. Now, tell me what's wrong, okay?"

But Juliet refused. "I need to look at you to talk right, and besides it's *private*," she insisted petulantly. "Vicki's right across the hall. She can hear me."

"So shut your door." Portia sighed, knowing what was coming.

"Mrs. Cousins says it's rude to shut the door in somebody's face, and Vicky's face is right there. She likes to listen to me talk on the phone. Portia, please come and pick me up and we can go and have doughnuts at Dunkin Donuts, okay? We can talk over a doughnut. Okay, Portia?"

Assessing over the phone whether there was a real emergency in Juliet's life, or how serious it might be, was impossible. The very last thing Portia wanted to do was drive across town and eat doughnuts. She'd had a chocolate bar for lunch and a handful of candies at some point during the afternoon. She was sugared out. She thought of a hot bath and bed.

Then she thought of how terrible she'd feel if Juliet did have an emergency.

"Okay, Jules, I'll be there in twenty minutes, but we're not having doughnuts. We'll go for a sub. I'm hungry."

I'm hungry—we're all going to eat. I'm tired— we're all going to bed early. Those were Lydia's lines. My God, was she turning into her mother?

"Okay, Portia, but I don't want them to put those hot things on my sub. Remember those hot green things I hate? Tell the man absolutely not to put them on. Okay, Portia? 'Cause I really hate them. Okay?"

"Yeah. Whatever. Okay, no green things. See you in twenty minutes."

Portia took time to scrub her face, hoping the cold rinse would wake her up, wondering if she could collapse into bed any time soon. She pulled on tights and a long sweater, and she was on her way out the door when she noticed the answering machine blinking again. She pressed the button.

"Hello, my fair lady." Nelson's deep voice was a little hesitant. "It's three in the afternoon and I've been thinking of you all day. I know you must be beat, and you need to go to bed early tonight, but I wanted to tell you—'' He hesitated, and she heard him swear under his breath when the words wouldn't come. ''Hell, I just wanted to tell you that I wish you were here with me right now. And that I meant what I said. If you ever need a sympathetic ear to bounce things off of, mine is available anytime.''

Portia told herself it was exhaustion that brought a lump to her throat....

Juliet was waiting on the steps of the group home when Portia drove up, and she could see by her sister's aura that she was agitated. Red flags of worry and anger and dark streaks of fear encircled her. She trotted down the sidewalk and wrenched open the passenger door before Portia could even shut off the motor, then tumbled inside in a clumsy flurry of arms and legs.

''Hi, Jules. Fasten your seat belt,'' Portia reminded her.

Juliet did, and then burst into tears.

''Hey, what is it, honey? What's wrong?'' Portia had been about to pull into traffic, but now she turned the ignition off.

''Stuart's mother and father are sending him away to live with his sister in Seattle,'' Juliet wailed.

"And his sister doesn't even want him. She doesn't like him, Stuart says. But his parents won't listen and he's going next week and now I'll never get to see him again and it's because his mother doesn't like me and my heart is hurting bad. And I called him just now because his mother is at bingo and I told him we'd meet him at the sub shop. He's gonna sneak out past his father. And you have to do something. Please, Portia."

Portia leaned over and put her aching forehead on the steering wheel. Dealing with Juliet was enough without having to contend with Stuart, as well.

She remembered Nelson's offer of a sympathetic ear, and for one desperate moment, she considered calling him and asking him to meet them at the sub shop. She abandoned it immediately.

Stuart was obsessed with cars, and once he laid eyes on the limo and found out Nelson was a race car driver, he'd be so distracted there wouldn't be a hope in Hades of getting him to discuss problems, much less solutions.

There was nothing for it except to forge ahead alone. She started the car and drove blearily to the sub shop.

Stuart was already there, standing off to one side of the entrance, rocking from one foot to the other.

He, too, was surrounded by colors that trumpeted his troubled emotions to Portia.

"There's Stuart. Hi, Stuart." Juliet bolted from the car, and the two threw their arms around each other and embraced as if they hadn't just spent the day working together.

"Hi, Dr. Portia." Stuart's round, florid face didn't have its usual beaming smile. Portia saw silver tear tracks on his cheeks as she returned the ferocious hug he gave her.

Inside, they finally got through the painfully slow process of ordering. Stuart had trouble coming to decisions, so it took forever for him to make up his mind about what he wanted. Juliet repeated her instructions about no hot peppers four times, Portia relayed her own order so quickly she had to go back over it, and through it all the patient young boy behind the counter, gangly and riddled with acne, smiled and nodded, doing his best to serve his customers.

In a booth at last, Portia unwrapped her sandwich and took a huge hungry bite.

Ordinarily, food was a major issue with both Juliet and Stuart, but tonight they simply sat close together, with their sandwiches still wrapped. They clung to each other's hands and looked at Portia as if she were the last hope they had in the world. But she was too hungry to get into their problems just yet. She washed her mouthful of veggie sub down with a swig of tea and took another bite.

"My mother will be mad at me when she finds I sneaked out," Stuart finally said in a worried tone. "I don't think I shoulda sneaked out, Juliet." He started to get up. "Maybe I should just go home now, before she gets back."

"But we need to talk, Stuart. You know we need to talk. Sit down." Juliet tugged his shirt, and he subsided into the booth.

Portia sighed and abandoned her sandwich for the time being. "Okay, guys. Tell me what the problems are and we'll see if we can find solutions, okay?"

Stuart: "My mother says I'm bad, she's sending me away—"

Juliet: "Stuart and I are gonna get married—"

Stuart: "I don't wanna go away—"

Juliet: "He's an adult. She can't do that—"

Their words and voices overlapped and Portia's head hurt more than ever.

"Okay, slow down and talk to me one at a time. Stuart, you go first."

But for several long moments, he couldn't talk. His eyes welled up with tears and he swallowed repeatedly and rocked on the seat. His huge hands, nails bitten to the quick, closed into fists, then opened and closed again.

"Let me tell her," Juliet interjected, but Portia stopped her.

"I need to have Stuart tell me how he feels," she told her sister. "You'll have your chance next. We have to take turns and be patient here, okay?"

Juliet subsided into a sulk.

"I gotta do what my mom says," Stuart blurted. "She says, she says, it's out of the question for me and Julie to get married. We're not—not—"

"*Capable*. She says we're not *capable*. But we are so," Juliet said. "We could get an apartment of our own. We both have jobs. We are so capable." She turned to Stuart. "I hate to say it, Stuart, but I don't like your mother. And I hate to say it, but she doesn't like me back. And I don't care, either."

Juliet's voice had gotten louder and louder, and Portia realized that people in adjoining booths and at the counter were looking. She was aware of their curiosity—their fear, too. They weren't sure what might happen next.

"I hate to say it, but your mother's a *bitch*," Juliet trumpeted.

"Hey, hey, let's calm down a little," Portia suggested. "Both of you take some deep breaths and together we'll try to think of what's best to do."

Which wasn't going to be easy—her brain felt as if it had gone on vacation without her.

They took her at her word, each drawing in huge breaths and expelling them with a whoosh.

"We could get married," Juliet suggested. "We could just go and get married, Stuart. We're old enough to get married, aren't we, Portia?"

"Yeah, you're both old enough." But Portia sensed the overwhelming fear that idea roused in Stuart. "It might not be the best solution, though, because it would make Stuart's family mad, and everyone needs their family behind them."

Stuart began to nod and couldn't stop. "Yeah, everyone needs their family. We don't want our family mad at us, right, Juliet?" His head bobbed like a child's toy. "It might not be the best solution."

"Your mother's mad, anyway, ever since I told her we have sex. Remember, Stuart? She's mad at me. She won't change even if we do get married." No one in the restaurant could help but hear Juliet.

Portia tried to change the subject. "Will you be able to get a job in Seattle, Stuart?"

"I dunno. I asked my mom, but she said, she said, 'That's not the issue here.'"

"Have you thought of moving out of your parents' house, maybe moving into a group home like Juliet?''

''I did, yeah, I thought and thought and thought about it.'' His hands clasped and unclasped, and his distress grew. ''But I'm not fit. My mother says I'm not fit. I can't buy my clothes. I can't cook. I dunno about banks and stuff like that.''

''That's just silly. You can learn. I learned all that stuff.'' Juliet blew a raspberry, but Portia heard the real fear in the young man's voice. Not that Stuart wasn't capable, but he was lacking self-confidence, and she couldn't see any way to bolster it. He'd have to acquire it on his own, as everyone did. And however much Juliet wanted marriage, bullying him into it wasn't the solution.

''Maybe you'll just have to go to Seattle, then, Stuart. Maybe you need time to think things through.''

Portia saw that Stuart was relieved, but she also saw the expression on Juliet's face. Her sister looked as if she'd just been betrayed by the person she most trusted.

Juliet gave Stuart a hard shove. ''Move. I need to get out.'' She scrambled out of the booth and flew out the door.

Portia caught up with her half a block down the street.

"You don't want me to be happy," Juliet hollered at her, fighting off Portia's efforts to put an arm around her. "Why'd you say that? You shouldn't have said that about Stuart going away."

"We can't be happy at someone else's expense, Jules. If Stuart isn't ready to take a stand on his own and marry you, then it's not right to force him."

"But I wanna be married to Stuart. I *love* Stuart." The declaration was a primal howl that echoed through the quiet evening.

Portia felt like howling herself. "We can't always have what we want, honey, not when it involves other people. They have to want it as much as we do."

"But Stuart loves me. He says he does all the time."

Portia sighed. "Saying and doing are different, Jules. He's not ready to get married. If he was, he'd stand up to his mother. I'm sorry, but that's the way it is."

Juliet was still sobbing, but now she allowed Portia to lead her to the car. Stuart was standing beside it, their subs gathered into a bundle and cradled in his hands.

"I brought you your sub, Juliet. You didn't eat your sub," he said in a conciliatory voice. "Don't cry, okay? It makes me cry, too, and men aren't s'posed to cry, right?''

"Go away, Stuart. I'm mad at you. I don't want to see you anymore."

He started rocking again. "Okay, okay, I'm going, but take your sub, okay? I gotta go home now, anyhow. My mom will really be mad at me. I'll see you at work tomorrow, okay, Juliet?" He shoved the sandwiches at Portia and then broke into a shambling run down the sidewalk.

"I hate him now. I love him, but I hate him, too," Juliet sobbed.

"Yeah, I've felt that way myself at times." Portia sighed. What woman hadn't? "Do you want to come and spend the night with me, Jules?" She started the car, visions of eight hours' sleep vanishing. Juliet would need to talk. And talk and talk and talk.

But her sister surprised her by shaking her head. "I wanna go home. I wanna be by my own self now."

Portia felt relieved, but guilty, as well. Juliet didn't say a word on the way back to the group home. She'd stopped crying by the time they arrived, and Portia gave her a hug before she got out of the car.

"Phone and let me know how you are, okay, Jules?"

"You're never there when I phone. I phoned and phoned you until it was late last night and you weren't there. Where were you, Portia?"

"I was with Nelson."

"At his house?"

"Yeah, at his house."

Juliet thought that over. "Were you *sleeping* with him?"

Portia sighed anew. She'd long ago made a pact with Juliet that they would be totally honest with each other, but at moments like this the promise was tough to stick to. "Yes, I was."

"Are you in love with Nelson?"

Honesty just got tougher and tougher around Juliet.

Portia groped for words.

"I..."

Was she in love with Nelson? The fact that she couldn't just deny it outright surprised her. "I'm not sure. It's too soon to tell."

"Does he have a mother?"

"Yeah, he does, but she doesn't live here. I think she's in Florida."

"Does she think you're a slut for sleeping with Nelson?"

"I've never met her, Jules." She could see where this conversation was leading. "Look, what Stuart's mother thinks of you isn't really important, any more than what Nelson's mother thinks of me. It's what we think of ourselves that matters. And what Stuart thinks of himself. And at the moment, I don't think he's strong enough to go against his mother's wishes."

Juliet nodded. "I know. But it still hurts in here." She put a hand flat on her chest. "And I have to go to the bathroom, too. So I'll leave now." She eyed the sandwiches on the seat. "Are you going to eat your submarine, Portia, or can I have it?"

"You take it. I'm not very hungry anymore." That her sister was thinking of her stomach again was a good sign.

Juliet gathered up the sandwiches and got out. She turned just before she went into the house and blew a forlorn kiss to Portia, and at that instant Portia caught a glimpse of her aura. The bright colors that normally surrounded Juliet were dull, shot through with gray and brown—visible signals of her distress.

Feeling as if she'd just gone ten rounds in a heavyweight boxing match, Portia drove home. Her heart ached for her sister. She had an overwhelming urge to drive to Stuart's house and spell out in vivid detail to the young man's mother exactly what damage she'd inflicted on her son's confidence and self-esteem with her overprotective, prissy attitudes and beliefs. For a perfectly normal person to have a healthy sense of self-worth was tough enough. For the mentally challenged, to whom so much of the world must seem an indecipherable puzzle, self-worth was hard-won. And from the sounds of it, Stuart hadn't had a fighting chance.

But antagonizing Mrs. Mays wouldn't help Juliet. And it wouldn't help Stuart, either. He had to somehow gain a sense of self-worth on his own. Then, and only then, would he be able to follow his heart.

Maybe if he spent time in Seattle he'd miss Juliet enough that he'd take control of his life. Maybe he'd even get brave enough to stand up to his mother.

And maybe, Portia thought as she pulled into her driveway, she oughta start writing romantic fairy tales. Stuart just wasn't very courageous, and going to Seattle wouldn't likely change that fact.

At this moment the only positive thing Portia could think of regarding Juliet and Stuart was that her sister had obviously given up on the idea of getting pregnant so that she and Stuart could get married.

Now, *that* idea had all the makings of a true disaster. Portia shuddered at the mere notion, although she well understood the feelings that had given birth to it. Love was an all-consuming and complex emotion, where too often the ends seemed to justify the means.

Inadvertently, her thoughts went to Nelson, and she wondered uneasily what the future held for the two of them.

One day at a time, she reminded herself.

Just take it one day at a time.

CHAPTER ELEVEN

AT LAST NELSON WAS ABLE to abandon the wheel-chair and graduate to crutches. Regaining mobility had become a full-time job, one to which he devoted time, energy and every ounce of determination he possessed.

"Most people need to be pushed to exercise," Charlie grumbled at him one rainy morning. "You're the only one who has therapists warning you to take it easy."

"Yeah, well maybe those folks don't have as much incentive as I do for getting back on their feet," Nelson said. "It's the middle of November. If I'm gonna drive in next summer's races, I've gotta get these damn muscles working."

Getting back on the circuit wasn't the only reason he had for fully recovering his strength, but his main objective wasn't one he was about to confide to Charlie. He fantasized constantly about being able to make love to Portia with no holds barred, wild and free and unhampered by his injuries.

Three weeks had gone by since that night they'd

first made love. Not more than three days had passed since without their making love again, but his desire for her wasn't diminished in the least. If anything, it was stronger than in the beginning, which constantly amazed him. Just thinking about her now brought a rush of powerful sexual energy, which he channeled into the task at hand.

Charlie hooked more weights to Nelson's ankles and stood back, a disapproving look on her face. "You've only been out of the wheelchair for three days. You're going at this rehab stuff way too hard, boss."

Right at this moment, Nelson thought so, too, but he wasn't about to admit it.

"That hip is gonna give you hell. It'll keep you from sleepin' tonight after this much of a workout," she predicted in her whispery voice.

"You were the one who told me the initials for physical therapy also stood for pain and torture," he puffed, face screwed into a grimace as he raised the weights and lowered them. Every muscle in his legs was screaming, and he didn't have to wait until bedtime for the hip to hurt. It already felt as if some sadistic son of a bitch was probing the joint with hot needles and electric shock. And his armpits hurt like fury from the damn crutches. Nobody had said how tough getting around on crutches would be. But they were a hell of an improvement over the wheel-

chair, he reminded himself with a shudder. He'd
come to despise that chair and the helplessness it
represented. He lowered the weights one last time
and knew he'd reached the limits of his endurance.

"How about making us a sandwich, Charlie? I'm
gonna shower and then I could stand some lunch."
He had a ton of paperwork to sort through this afternoon before he met Portia. She wouldn't be done
her shift at St. Joe's until four, and then they were
picking up Juliet and taking her out to dinner.

"You want ham on rye? Or tuna on whole
wheat?"

"Ham." He grinned at her. "And then maybe a
coupla tuna as a chaser—I'm starving."

He grabbed the crutches and headed for the
shower, reflecting on the past three weeks. After that
first memorable night, he'd half expected Portia to
run. He wasn't certain why. Maybe it had to do with
how elusive she'd been at the start. He still was
never quite sure she'd go out with him again.

There was also the lovemaking itself. For the first
time in his life, his partner had had to do all the
physical stuff. He'd never felt as vulnerable and insecure about himself as he had that night, and he'd
never experienced such erotic intensity. He still
couldn't bring himself to believe that the sex was
as explosive for her as it was for him.

The day after they'd first made love, he'd gotten

tickets to *Les Misérables,* hardly daring to hope that she'd accompany him, but she had. And she'd made it clear that she wanted to go to bed with him again. Probably not quite as much as he wanted to take her there, he mused with a wry grin.

They'd grown more comfortable with each other during the past several weeks. He'd even confided how it felt to have her do all the work during love-making. She'd laughed and warned him that he wasn't going to get away with it much longer, no matter how much he liked it.

Best of all, for three solid weeks he'd hardly thought about Huntington's. Whether Portia was beside him or not, he slept peacefully and awakened each morning without the emotional heaviness he'd become accustomed to, the fear that each new day meant being one day closer to the disease.

Instead, his waking thoughts had been of Portia, and the mornings she was there beside him were blissful.

He whistled as he showered. Charlie had lunch on the table by the time he was dressed, and Nelson ate his way through a stack of sandwiches. His appetite was back, and he'd started to regain the weight he'd lost since his accident. He downed a glass of grapefruit juice and was reaching for one of the oatmeal cookies Charlie had arranged on a small plate when he noticed she wasn't eating.

"You not feeling well?" He knew she wasn't on a diet. One of the things he really liked about her was that she never appeared to worry about what she weighed. Charlie and Portia were the only two women he'd ever met who seemed free of weight phobia.

She shook her head, glancing up at him from under her lashes. "I need to talk to you, Nelson."

Charlie hardly ever used his name. She called him "boss," or "honey" or "sweetie." This must be serious.

"Go ahead. I'm listening."

"There's, um…I've, uh, I've realized that, uh, I guess, well, the fact is, I've—oh hell." Her face was flushed and her eyes were downcast. She was clutching her coffee mug so tight her knuckles were white.

Warning bells went off in Nelson's head and horror filled him, along with a strong premonition that she was about to tell him she'd fallen in love with him. God, how would he handle this without hurting her?

"See, I know this job is almost over. You'll be getting your casts off and driving yourself soon. You're already on crutches. You don't really need me anymore."

It was true. In another week, two at the most, he planned to be independent.

"I've enjoyed working for you more than I ever enjoyed a job before." Charlie's fluttery little voice was choked with emotion, and Nelson wished with every fiber of his being that he were somewhere else. He hated having to tell women that whatever it was they felt for him, he didn't feel the same.

"See, I loved the chauffeur part of it, driving you around in that big car. And it dawned on me, how I felt about..."

Here it came. Nelson's throat was dry, and the sandwiches weren't sitting well in his gut.

"...about driving. I've always loved driving, and I wondered...do you think there's any chance maybe—" her already soft voice dropped so low he had to lean forward to hear it "—maybe I could start my own business? There must be lots of people around in wheelchairs who need a service that provides transportation and a driver with medical knowledge."

His ego needed a moment to recover. He swallowed and then said feebly, "Business? You want to start your own business?"

"I knew I shouldn't have even mentioned it. I knew it was crazy. What do I know about starting a business?" Her face crumpled and tears trickled out of her blue eyes. "Forget I ever said anything. It's a stupid idea. I don't have much money. There's no way I could."

"But it's not crazy, not at all. Hey, Charlie, please don't cry. It's just—I didn't have any idea what you were going to ask me. It's a surprise, that's all." He thought for a moment. "Y'know, you might really be on to something here."

The tears stopped. She sniffled, blew her nose, gave him a wary look.

"Really?"

"I'd have to do some market research, but when I called around for cars that could handle wheelchairs, the only ones available were those taxicabs with the bubble tops. The limo companies said they'd send a strong driver who'd transfer me from my chair into the limo, but I'd never have chanced that—I'm not exactly ninety pounds. Besides, getting picked up and put down is humiliating."

"You had your limo adapted for your chair. What're you going to do with it now?"

"I hadn't really thought about it."

"Would you—d'ya think you might sell it?" She gulped and whispered, "To me?"

"Absolutely. You'd have to get a business license and probably upgrade your driver's license, but I'll find out exactly what you need. As for the limo, we'll work something out, like a lease to buy, so you can pay as you go."

"You'd do that for me? Oh, Nelson, gosh, thanks.

Thank you.'' She leaped up and enveloped him in a hug that came close to breaking his ribs.

"I'll get on it right away. You need to find a name for your company.''

"I've tried. I can't come up with one that sounds good. If you were starting the business, what would you call it?''

Nelson thought for a moment. "Low Rider.'' The words had stuck in Nelson's mind, and he'd made a point of searching out War, the group who had first used them.

He punched the song into the remote CD player.

"Low Rider Limo Service. Take a little trip with me. Oh, I love it. It's perfect,'' Charlie breathed. "Nelson, you're brilliant.''

"Not me. But I'll pass along the compliment to Cedric.''

"He's a sweet guy, isn't he?'' Charlie had driven Nelson, Cedric and Gordon out to the track the week before for the ride Nelson had promised them in his race car. The elation on Cedric's face afterward had made Nelson feel humble. It had been such a small thing to him, but to Cedric it had been a once-in-a-lifetime experience.

For the next hour, Nelson answered the excited questions that Charlie shot at him, everything from how to keep books for a small business to advice on advertising. Nelson was no expert at small-business management, but he had contacts who were, and he put Charlie in touch with them.

Charlie finally tore herself away and went out to buy groceries, and Nelson sat at the computer, trying to concentrate on his own business, tracking spreadsheets and market predictions, but he felt restless and impatient with the slow progress of his healing, and the restrictions it put on his life.

He needed something active, something physical, something that occupied his attention the way racing had while he waited for his body to heal. He'd made a list once of things he'd wanted to accomplish before—

Before.

He called the list up on his laptop, and there, number seven, was the perfect solution.

Flying. He'd always wanted to learn how to fly a small craft, and there was no reason he couldn't begin now. His arms were stronger than they'd ever been. And as long as he could struggle into the plane, his hip wouldn't be too much of an impediment.

He grabbed the Yellow Pages and looked up flight schools, and within half an hour, he'd made arrangements for his first lesson.

He hung up the phone with a familiar feeling of

anticipation and excitement. He couldn't wait to start.

He couldn't wait to tell Portia.

"I LIKE MY CAR FINE, but I do miss driving the limo," Portia said.

They were in her Datsun, heading for Juliet's. Now that Nelson didn't need the wheelchair, getting around was much easier, but Portia had become used to handling the sleek, big car when she and Nelson went out. There was something so decadent about piloting the vehicle through Vancouver traffic. No one messed with a limousine, and Portia enjoyed the feeling of power.

"Maybe Charlie'll let us borrow it now and then." Nelson then explained about the business Charlie was determined to start.

"What a great idea. She should put an ad for the service on the bulletin board at St. Joe's." Portia turned and smiled at him, thinking that he was more handsome than ever now that his energy and strength were improving. "Sounds like you two had a productive afternoon."

"Must have been something in the phase of the moon, because I also figured out what I want to do with my spare hours until I'm fully mobile again. Besides making love with you, that is." And then he told her about registering for flying lessons.

She swallowed hard and made an effort to look receptive, but she felt horrified.

"Isn't that a pretty dangerous hobby?"

"No more so than anything else I've done."

"I suppose not." Confusing emotions tumbled through her. She felt disappointed, let down, vaguely angry with him. She tried to figure out exactly why as she maneuvered through traffic. It had something to do with confirming her fears about him.

"I'll take you up as soon as I've got my license."

"I don't think so." She shook her head. "I'm a nervous passenger. I don't like flying in commercial planes. I sure as heck wouldn't be comfortable in a small one."

"Even with me as pilot?" His tone was teasing, but she had the feeling something more serious was behind it.

"Well, your track record as a pilot isn't exactly reassuring, if we factor in race cars." She kept her tone light, too, but she felt he was pressuring her, and she didn't like it.

"You don't trust me. You're breaking my heart." He made his voice sound comically pathetic, but again she knew that he wasn't entirely joking. Not that his heart was breaking. But she intuitively saw that he wanted her to trust him.

"Better your heart broken than your body." Yet

what about *her* heart? Wasn't that what these feelings were all about? She'd never allowed herself to admit it, but on some level, she'd been hoping she and Nelson had a future together.

Trust went both ways. She'd wanted him to trust her intuition about the Huntington's, give up his fears, move on and stop risking life and limb by pursuing dangerous sports. Obviously, it had been too much to want.

He started talking about Charlie again, and how they'd come up with the name for the company, and by the time he was done, they were at the group home.

Portia pulled up at the curb, but Juliet didn't come tearing out the way she normally did.

"Wait here a minute. I'll go get her."

Portia ran up the walk and knocked.

"Hello, Dr. Bailey."

"Hello, Mrs. Cousins." Portia had long ago given up trying to get on a more casual basis with the portly woman. She exchanged the usual comments on the weather and then said, "Is Juliet ready?"

"She was down here fifteen minutes ago, but she's disappeared again. Why don't you go up to her room and see what's keeping her. She's been complaining of a touch of stomach flu this past week. Did she tell you?"

Juliet hadn't said anything on the phone, which wasn't like her. Portia climbed the stairs and walked along the hallway to her sister's door, which was closed. She tapped and called and then tried the handle. It released, and she went in.

"Jules? You ready to go to dinner?" She hadn't seen Juliet for a week, but they'd talked on the phone every other day.

Stuart had left for Seattle ten days ago, and Portia was relieved that Juliet seemed to be adjusting to his absence. She still spoke about him all the time, but she'd stopped crying when she mentioned him.

The door to the bathroom was shut, and Portia could hear water running. She waited a few minutes and then knocked.

"Jules? You okay?"

"I'm brushing my teeth. I'm okay now. I'm coming, Portia." The door opened at last and Juliet came out, drying her mouth on the corner of a blue towel. The acrid smell of vomit surrounded her. "I had to throw up. I threw up three times already today."

"Ah, Jules, you're sick, honey. Why didn't you call me? What's—"

And suddenly Portia knew. She saw it in the aura around her sister, in the transparency of her skin, the fragility of her expression, and wondered with a sinking feeling how she could have missed it a week ago. But she hadn't been looking; she'd thought it was no longer a possibility. And she was trying so hard these days not to look at people that way anymore.

She groaned, "Oh, God, Jules." A sense of absolute horror swept over her. "When did you last have a period?"

"It's late. It should have come two weeks ago, but it didn't."

"Juliet, you're pregnant, aren't you?"

"Can you see the baby?" Juliet's skin was pale, and she appeared drawn and tired, but her ecstatic smile stretched from ear to ear. "You can *see* it, in my colors, can't you, Portia? When I missed my period, I didn't know for sure. I was gonna ask you, but now I don't need to, right? Can you see if it's a boy or a girl? I so much want a girl, but I think when Stuart knows he'll want a boy. Oh, Portia, I'm so *excited*," she crowed. "It's making me throw up all the time, and I'm very, very, very dizzy. And very, very, very sleepy. But that's okay, isn't it, Portia? That's just the baby growing, isn't it, Portia?"

Speechless, Portia collapsed on a chair beside Juliet's bed as a whole new set of confusing emotions tumbled through her—anger, frustration, dismay. And resentment, loud and clear.

Like it or not, Juliet's pregnancy would drastically affect her own life. The baby would be her niece or nephew, and there was no way she could refuse to be involved in its life, no way she'd *want* to refuse. She loved her sister; she'd love the child. But with Juliet as a mother, the baby would need so much support, demand so much time—time she didn't have to give.

Portia tried to control her voice, but she didn't succeed. "I thought we agreed that you wouldn't do this, Juliet. I thought you understood it would be a mistake to get pregnant."

"You're mad at me." Juliet stood in the center of her bedroom, agitated, waving clasped hands.

Portia looked from her sister to the row of dolls on the window seat, dolls that Juliet still played with. Had her sister begun to understand how different babies were from dolls? "Jules? I thought you promised me."

Juliet gave her head a prolonged and vigorous shake. "Uh-uh, I didn't. Nope, that's not how it was. *You* said it was a mistake, but I didn't say okay. I never said I wouldn't. Remember how I never said? I didn't promise you, and I have to use my own judgment about my body. Remember you told me that lots of times. And I did. I used my own judgment, and I'm glad, so there." Her face crumpled. "I don't want you to be mad at me, though. Don't be mad at me, okay, Portia? Okay?" Her chin wobbled and her arms moved faster and faster.

Portia was beyond anger. She felt like bursting into tears. She felt like walking out, abandoning Juliet, dealing only with her own life for once, instead of constantly rescuing and caring for her sister. The ramifications of Juliet's pregnancy ran through her mind, each one far-reaching, each one affecting her own life in ways even she couldn't totally imagine.

"Oh boy oh boy. You're really mad at me. Don't be mad, Portia. You'll like it when I get the baby. I know you will. You like babies, right?"

Portia felt aged and weary and defeated.

"Get your coat on, Jules. Nelson's waiting for us in the car." If there was one thing she'd learned from Juliet, it was that regrets were useless. Her only real option was to deal with the situation here and now, without dwelling on regrets.

"But you're mad at me. It makes me feel bad when you're mad at me."

Portia sighed and forced a strained smile. "I'm not mad, honey. I'm concerned about you. I'm in shock. But I'm not mad, okay?"

Juliet leaned close and studied her sister's face for a moment, and, apparently reassured by what she saw, nodded. "Okay. Where are we going for supper, Portia? I don't want to go for Chinese. The smell makes me feel sick. Even when I walk past that place near the bakery, you know the one with the big dragon, it makes me feel like I'm going to throw up.''

"No Chinese. We're going to Hamburger Heaven, downtown.''

"I love burgers, but will they have fries? Because I really want fries, with gravy. Not ketchup, gravy, okay?''

Portia helped her into her coat. Juliet held her hand as they went down the stairs. Mrs. Cousins was still in the downstairs hall, and she asked Juliet if she was feeling better.

"I had to throw up, but I'm okay now. We're going to eat at Hamburger Heaven downtown, where they have fries and gravy," Juliet told her.

"Enjoy yourselves." Mrs. Cousins smiled.

"We will, won't we, Portia?''

Portia forced another smile and agreed, wondering if Mrs. Cousins had any suspicions about what was making Juliet sick. She probably did; the house-mother was far more perceptive than she seemed, and of course Juliet would blurt out the news soon. It was a wonder she hadn't already.

Harmony House was a small privately owned facility, one of the best in the city. There was a long waiting list to get in, and the rules were strict. Babies weren't allowed, so Juliet would have to move out.

Move where? Her sister wasn't capable of living alone.

With a weary sigh, Portia decided she'd think about it all later. It had been a long day, and she was hungry.

Nelson was waiting, not so patiently. "Hi, Juliet." He grinned at her as she climbed into the back seat. "Don't brain yourself on my crutches. What took you two so long? I'm dying of starvation here."

Juliet slammed the car door and concentrated on fastening her seat belt before she answered. "I had to vomit and then I cleaned my teeth, and then Portia looked at my colors, and guess what?"

Portia started the car and pulled into the rush-hour traffic, then snapped, "Juliet, that whole subject is private, okay?" She felt like clamping a hand over her sister's mouth. Not that she didn't want Nelson to know; she'd tell him herself, but just not here and not now. She really didn't want to go through the conversation all over again. She needed time to digest it, to come to terms with it, whatever terms were possible.

"You are *so* mad at me, Portia. You said you weren't, but you are." Juliet burst into noisy tears. "I want to stay home. I don't want to go to Hamburger Heaven. Not with you, Portia. You're mean to me."

"Juliet, for God's sake, shut up. I'm not mad, okay?" Portia's store of patience was gone. She knew she sounded exasperated. She certainly felt that way. "And I'm not taking you home. We're already halfway there. I can't turn around here, anyway. We're in the wrong lane." She wasn't making things any better, but for once she just didn't care.

Nelson did his best to smooth the situation. "Hey, sweetheart, don't cry," he cajoled Juliet. "You have to come to dinner. I've made the reservations. We can't cancel at this late date, can we? Hamburger Heaven knows you're coming. I told them to have a good supply of fries and gravy."

Nelson pulled a handful of tissues from the box Portia kept handy and gave them to Juliet. When Portia glanced over at him, he raised an eyebrow and spread his hands questioningly.

"Don't ask," she muttered, maneuvering through downtown traffic and then driving around the block three times before she found a parking spot.

By the time she'd calmed Juliet and they were finally seated in the popular eating place, Portia was the one who wanted nothing more than to go home. Juliet looked woebegone, but she also looked ill. There was a faint greenish tinge to her skin, and her hands trembled when she studied the menu, which had colorful pictures of all the selections.

They ordered, and when the beverages came, Juliet drank two glasses of water and then her tall soda, barely pausing for breath.

"I'm thirsty all the time, and I have to pee lots," she stage-whispered to Portia, leaning over the table and using her hand to block her words from Nelson. "Is that because the baby's inside water?"

Of course Nelson heard her. Portia saw the surprise and shock on his face as recognition dawned. The look he shot Portia was sympathetic.

"When are you going to tell Stuart you're pregnant, Jules?" Portia gave up. There was no point now attempting to direct the conversation elsewhere.

"When he phones me. He goes to a pay phone on a corner by a gas station and he phones me collect, but he can't always. I can't call him because his sister won't let him talk to me. His mother says I'm a bad influ—infru—"

"Influence," Portia supplied with a sigh.

"Influence, yeah." Juliet clapped a hand over her mouth. "O-o-o-oh, you forgot. You said me being pregnant was private, and now you told Nelson."

"I think he guessed."

Juliet smiled at him. "You're really smart, aren't you, Nelson?"

"We're all smart in some ways and not so smart in others," he replied.

The waiter came with their food, but Portia's appetite had disappeared. She toyed with her salad and tried not to think about all the serious problems Juliet's pregnancy would create. She was sitting beside Nelson, and he reached under the table and gave her leg a squeeze. When she looked at him, he winked and smiled. She should have felt reassured, but she didn't.

Juliet wasn't his sister. He might sympathize, but in the end Juliet's issues weren't his to deal with. He had his own demons to face. But at least he could make decisions about his life without considering anyone except himself. He *did* make decisions that way. She remembered the flying lessons, and her spirits sank even lower.

Juliet's appetite had resurfaced, and she ate hungrily and chattered between mouthfuls about her baby and the clothes she planned to get for it and the names she liked. Nelson listened and answered her questions and didn't ask any.

After what seemed an eternity to Portia, they finished the meal and drove Juliet home. She gave them each a hug before she got out of the car.

"I'll call you on the phone tomorrow, Portia, okay?"

"Yeah. I'll be at work, but I'll leave my cell phone open."

"Don't forget, okay? Remember that time you promised and then you forgot."

Portia assured her she wouldn't. "I'm going to get you an appointment with a friend of mine, a special lady doctor who knows everything about babies. Okay, Jules?"

Juliet hated seeing doctors, a result of her early childhood when Lydia had hauled her from one to the other, searching for a miracle.

"Do I have to? Will you come with me, Portia?"

"Absolutely."

"Okay, but only if you come with me."

Portia waited until Juliet was in the house before she drove away.

Nelson sat quietly beside her for several blocks, and then he said, "That must have been a hell of a shock for you."

"Yeah, it was." Portia concentrated on her driving. "I'd rather not talk about it, if you don't mind."

The atmosphere between them was strained. Portia knew it was her doing, and again she didn't care. When they reached his building, she pulled up in front instead of heading into the garage.

"You're not coming up?" His disappointment was evident.

She shook her head. "Not tonight." She didn't make any excuses and he didn't ask for any.

He leaned over and tried to take her in his arms, but the small space made it difficult. He cupped her head in his palms and drew her close enough to kiss, and for a moment she regretted not going up with him.

The sexual attraction between them was intense, as always. Making love would drive everything out of her mind, at least for a while. She almost said she'd stay, but she couldn't get the words out. She needed to be alone.

"'Night, sweetheart." Nelson stroked her cheek with the back of his fingers. "If you want to talk, call. Any hour at all, I'm here."

She thanked him, helped him out of the car, then drove away, but she didn't go home. She had to keep moving, to put off the time when she'd have to think rationally.

She drove fast, mindlessly, through the city, around the park, along the waterfront, pop music blaring on the radio. A despondency so overwhelming she didn't know what to do to ease it filled her. She needed to talk to someone impartial and understanding, someone who knew her and knew the complications of her life.

There was only one person.

Her tires screeched as she pulled to the side of the road. She dug her cell phone out of her bag and dialed Joanne Mathews's number from memory.

Mercifully, Joanne answered, and within minutes, Portia was heading for the west side of the city.

CHAPTER TWELVE

"I FEEL TERRIBLE BARGING IN on you like this."
Portia balanced the mug of tea Joanne handed her
and sank back into the colorful down pillows strewn
across the dove-gray sofa.

Joanne and Spence had bought a large old three-
story house after the twins came. They were now
remodeling. Spence had redone the original oak
floors, and Joanne had laid down vivid jewel-toned
wool rugs, their rich hues echoing those of the sofa
pillows. With its soft lamps, gas fireplace, aubergine
walls and intriguingly offbeat artwork, the room was
at once relaxing and enriching to the senses. The
brightly colored crooked tower of plastic building
blocks beside the sofa and the small red tricycles in
the corner added to the cozy ambience.

"I wish you'd do this more often," Joanne insisted, sitting down beside Portia. "And you're in
luck. It's Spence's turn to put the gremlins to bed."

"I love what you've done with this room," Portia
remarked. "If you ever gave up on the ER, you

could easily make millions as an interior decorator.''

"Not enough of an adrenaline rush," Joanne said. "Besides, I don't have any idea what other people like. I only do what I want." She grinned. "That's selfish, but Spence is an easygoing guy when it comes to decorating."

Squeals and a thundering on the stairs signaled the arrival of the twins. They shot around the corner and into the room, two sturdy three-year-olds with wet black hair, their bodies as bare as the day they'd been born. They were holding hands and giggling. When they spied Portia, they stopped running. Jade-green eyes, their mother's eyes, widened behind long lashes.

"Didn't know we had company, did you, you nudists? Say hello to Portia," Joanne instructed, and in tandem they caroled a cheerful greeting.

"Where are your pajamas?" Joanne shook her head and rolled her eyes at Portia. "This is a new game. They call it hiding on Daddy, for some unknown reason."

"Hide on Daddy," Lillianna crowed.

"Hide on Daddy," her brother, Benjamin, parroted, and he snatched the throw from the sofa, crouched in the corner and pulled it over his head. Lillianna wriggled behind a chair. More giggles escaped from each of them.

"Here you are, you wicked rascals." Spence looked as if he'd taken a bath with his jeans and T-shirt on. "Hi, Portia."

He made an elaborate pretense of searching before he finally found his son and daughter. "I'm sure you won't mind if we disappear back upstairs." He scooped up the twins, one wriggling body under each muscular arm, and held them reasonably still for Joanne to kiss.

"I'll do my best, but I can't promise they'll stay in bed," he warned her.

"They will if you don't fall asleep before they do," Joanne stated. "It's just a matter of stamina."

"Easy for you to say." With a grin, Spence headed up the steps with his squirming cargo, and Joanne sighed. "I've come to the conclusion that endurance is the answer to child raising. Those two would wear out a saint." She took a sip of tea and eyed Portia questioningly.

"You didn't come over here to talk about kids, though. I can tell something's bothering you. What is it?"

"Just about everything." Portia set her cup down and folded her arms across her chest. "I don't even know where to begin."

"Have you fallen in love with that race car driver?" Joanne was aware that Portia had been seeing a lot of Nelson.

Portia remembered Juliet asking her the same question not too long ago. She'd said that she didn't know. She opened her mouth to tell Joanne the same thing, but instead she heard herself say, "Yeah. Yeah, I have, damn it all to hell."

"You make it sound like a fate worse than death."

"That's exactly what it feels like," Portia admitted. "He's a rich playboy who's never gonna settle down. He goes from one toy to the other. Because he can't race cars at the moment, he's decided to fly airplanes. When that novelty wears off and his hip heals, he'll probably trek off to Nepal or somewhere. And it's inevitable that he'll get bored with me and move on. I'm a novelty at the moment, but that'll change." She shook her head in despair. "I'm such an idiot. I knew from the beginning I shouldn't fall for him, but I let my guard down for one second and it happened."

"I'm convinced there aren't any mistakes in the universe," Joanne said. "You can't ever predict what another person will do, or what he's feeling. Try not to worry about what the future holds. Just enjoy each day and leave it at that."

"Easier said than done." Portia herself had handed out the exact advice so many times. "I guess I'm a coward about my heart. I don't look forward to getting it broken."

Joanne smiled. "I remember thinking precisely that when I fell in love with Spence. He told me right up front there was no chance for us—he was never going to get married again."

"He did?" Portia was astonished. She'd always believed Joanne and Spence had had a fairy-tale courtship. They certainly had a happy marriage.

"Sure he did. And I believed him. I went off by myself on that horrible cruise to Alaska, and when I got back, he came to his senses." Joanne's eyes twinkled. "Men just aren't too bright when it comes to matters of the heart. They're wired differently than we are. You have to overlook what they say and instead gauge what they're feeling. And you have an inside track on that, because you can tell by their colors, right?"

Portia blew out an exasperated breath. "I guess that's another one of the reasons I'm crying on your shoulder. You know since Betty Hegard died that I've been trying not use my psychic ability at work."

Joanne nodded and waited.

"It's just so damn hard not to," Portia burst out. "Instead of being able to relax and enjoy the job the way I used to, I find myself with a headache at the end of the day from the stress of trying not to *see*."

"That's something you'll have to come to terms

with," Joanne said. "It sounds as if you're not being true to yourself. Personally, I view your ability to diagnose through seeing as an extraordinary gift."

It was Portia's turn to nod. Joanne had always encouraged her to use her gift in the ER. But Joanne was no longer senior ER physician at St. Joe's; she'd relinquished the position so she could work only part-time and raise her family. The man who'd taken her place, Dr. Hudson, was older, a by-the-book physician who opposed anything that smacked of alternative medicine. And the hospital board supported his views; they'd been explicit about that when they'd reprimanded Portia in the Betty Hegard inquiry.

Joanne was well aware of all this. "You may find you have to look elsewhere for a place to best use your abilities," she said softly.

The thought had crossed Portia's mind more than once, and it always depressed her. "But I love St. Joe's. It's like home to me."

"We all have to leave home eventually." Joanne's words were gentle, but the reality of them hit Portia hard.

"More tea?" Joanne filled their cups. "So besides work and your love life, what else is falling apart? There's a universal law that says we can't deal with merely one or two problems at a time."

"You're dead-on," Portia admitted. "I feel awful dumping all my troubles on you, but I can't seem to help myself. There's also Juliet." She drew in a deep breath and let it out in a whoosh. "My sister's pregnant. I just found out tonight."

"Oh, dear." Joanne knew Juliet well; the three women had gone to lunch occasionally. "Is the father supportive?"

Portia shook her head and explained about Stuart. "They care for each other, but he's just not emotionally strong. I'm certain Juliet's going to go through this without him. He's living in Seattle."

"It puts an enormous burden on you. I don't suppose your mother—"

"Nope. We haven't told her she's about to become a grandmother, but my guess is she'll be conspicuous by her absence, as usual."

Joanne had also met Lydia. She nodded reluctant agreement. "I don't suppose abortion is an option?"

"Nope. Juliet is thrilled and wouldn't think of aborting. I'm a lot less enthusiastic. She's already suggested that she and the baby move in with me."

"That's not an option, of course. But I see what you're up against. It's tough to be a parent, even with no disability and a husband to share the duties. Alone and mentally challenged..." Joanne trailed off. "It's tough on Juliet, but it's doubly hard on you, Portia."

Portia felt tears well up at Joanne's understanding and sympathy. Being able to share how she felt was such a relief. She told Joanne so.

"If there's anything at all that I can do, *anything,* you have only to ask." Joanne reached across and took Portia's hand. "I wish there were something immediate and practical that would make everything easier, but I can't think what." She squeezed Portia's hand. "Unless you want me to tell Spence to have a heart-to-heart with Nelson Gregory and ask him his intentions?" She giggled at the absolute horror on Portia's face. "And when he's done that, we could get him to talk to Stuart's mother, as well."

It was good to laugh. Portia felt better, even though nothing had changed. She and Joanne chatted about work for another half hour, and then Portia left, promising to have lunch with Joanne soon and to keep her posted on what was happening.

"I feel like a character in a soap opera," Portia remarked as Joanne gave her a hug at the door.

"Not just a character, honey," Joanne said with a grin. "You're the star."

Portia was still smiling as she drove home. If she was the star, then she should have some say in the action. She glanced at her watch. It was just past eleven. She fumbled her cell phone out of her bag and tapped in another number she knew off by heart.

She'd begin by calling Nelson and apologizing for having been such a bitch tonight.

WHEN THE PHONE RANG Nelson snatched it up, half expecting it to be the Florida doctor he'd spoken to an hour earlier. He steeled himself for what could only be bad news.

"Nelson?"

"God, Portia, I'm so glad it's you." He slumped onto the bed, shoving his partially filled suitcase out of the way.

"So who were you expecting, the drug squad?" Her voice was relaxed and filled with warmth and humor.

"I was afraid it might be my mother's doctor. My mom's just had a severe heart attack. She's asking for me, and he said that it would be wise for me to get there as quickly as possible. I called the airlines. There's a seat available on a flight leaving at midnight, so I'm packing. I was going to call you as soon as everything was arranged."

"Oh, Nelson, I'm so sorry. Can I do anything? Do you need a ride to the airport?"

"Not if you're in bed already. I can call a cab."

"I'm in the car, not far from your apartment. I'll be there in a few minutes."

She rang off, and he felt better. He didn't question

why that was so; he only knew it comforted him to have her with him, have her drive him to the airport.

Hearing that his mother was ill had been a shock. Now he felt troubled, worried and guilty and anxious. He hadn't seen her for more than a year. He was grateful that at least he was out of the wheelchair. He was still on crutches, though, and if his mother was conscious, she'd be horrified and hurt that he hadn't told her about his own health misfortunes.

He'd distanced himself from his mother for a good reason—he didn't want her feeling responsible for him if—when—the Huntington's appeared. But he'd felt lonely without her in his life, Nelson admitted to himself as he folded shirts and tossed underwear into his case. Madeleine Gregory had been a wonderful mother, loving and funny and warm. Nelson knew that his self-imposed estrangement had hurt her. She'd made innumerable efforts over the years to bridge the distance he'd created, but he'd always resisted her overtures, telling himself it was for her own good.

The buzzer sounded, and as he hurried to let Portia in, he hoped against hope that if Madeleine was going to die, it wouldn't happen before he got to her. He needed to say things to her, ask her things.

Most important, he needed to tell her he loved her.

Not for her sake, but for his.

PORTIA WATCHED AS NELSON made his way through
the security check. He stopped on the far side and
waved to her, and there was something so forlorn
in his expression that all of a sudden she wished
she'd had the courage to do more than just wish
him good luck and kiss him goodbye. She should
have told him how much she cared about him,
maybe even said straight out that she loved him.

Then again, maybe not. If she'd done so, he'd
probably feel he had to say something similar back,
and the last thing she wanted was a trade-last.

He hadn't talked much about his mother on the
way to the airport. Portia had asked a few questions,
but it was obvious Nelson didn't want to discuss
her, just as Portia earlier hadn't wanted to talk about
Juliet. So they'd made idle conversation about the
rain, about how nice it would be for Nelson to soak
up some Florida sunshine. Portia told him about the
twins and their nudist tendencies, about Joanne's
talents as a decorator. Nelson talked about Cedric
and how much he seemed to have enjoyed the time
at the racetrack.

There'd been the usual controlled confusion at the
airport with getting tickets and checking bags. Then
he'd kissed her, holding her close for a long, des-

perate moment. When he was gone, Portia felt bereft.

THE FEELING INTENSIFIED the following morning when Gordon Caldwell, Cedric's nurse, stopped by the ER and asked if she'd come to an emergency meeting he'd called about Cedric.

"I went to see him this morning," Gordon said. "He's got a cold. As you know, ALS patients often die from mucous buildup they can't clear away themselves, and his muscles are already very weak. This could well develop into pneumonia unless something's done. He wouldn't let me bring him into Emerg, but I could see that he was feeling pretty rough."

The ER was quiet, and Portia hurried down the hall with Gordon to the small meeting room. The hospital's palliative care supervisor, Vanessa Thorpe, was there, as well as Dr. Melvin Halliday, the neurologist caring for him.

Gordon explained his concerns, and then Halliday gave his professional opinion.

"Cedric's condition is worsening much faster than anticipated, in my opinion due in part to his living conditions. I would recommend that he be brought as soon as possible into the Palliative Care Unit," Halliday stated. "These things are difficult to predict accurately, but my most optimistic guess is that Mr. Vencour has only six to eight weeks left to live."

Portia had known, of course, but hadn't wanted to face up to how quickly Cedric was deteriorating. Her heart ached for her friend. "Gordon and I have both tried to convince Cedric to come in for palliative care," she said with a sigh, "but he refuses. He insists he wants to die in his own place. The lack of water or bathroom facilities must be making it impossible for Gordon to care for him properly."

Gordon agreed. "I'm doing my best, but there's only so much I can do, given the circumstances." He cleared his throat and glanced at Vanessa Thorpe. "I've been thinking about it," he continued in a tentative voice. "He lives in a packing box. Why can't we just move it into one of the palliative care rooms and let him go on living in it? That way he'd have access to a bathroom and the care he needs, but he'd be in his own place. He might agree to do it on those terms."

"Gordon, that's brilliant." Portia was excited. "How big is the box?"

"About eight feet by eight."

"It would fit. Those rooms are bigger than that." Portia was already rearranging furniture in her mind. "With the bed gone, there'd be plenty of room."

But Vanessa was shaking her head. "My concern

is what sort of germs would we be bringing in? The nurses would object on those grounds, I'm sure."

Gordon's quiet demeanor didn't change, but his voice became firmer. "In-hospital palliative care means that people aren't looking at getting well, so germs are not a major concern here. I'll make sure his clothes and his sleeping bag are laundered. The only other things he has are books and a radio. We could put him in one of those end rooms near the door. That way his friends could visit easily. I checked just now. The one on the right is empty."

Vanessa was still shaking her head.

In her excitement at Gordon's idea, Portia had forgotten her vow not to look at auras. She could see the disturbance in Vanessa's colors, a particular shade of blue that indicated a conservative nature and a dedication to duty. It didn't take psychic ability to recognize that Vanessa was cautious in word, action and dress.

"It's just not possible," she declared, confirming Portia's assessment. "Infection control is very much an issue here."

Portia wanted to shake her, remind her that Cedric wasn't infectious. So he brought in a few fleas. Surely the hospital had disinfectants powerful enough to deal with them.

"Well, it sounds like a good idea to me," Dr. Halliday said, gathering up his briefcase and notes.

"But of course it's up to Vanessa. If you'll excuse me, I have a patient waiting." He hurried out the door.

Coward, Portia screamed silently at his retreating back. As Cedric's neurologist, he could have been a lot more supportive and insistent.

"I can see it would solve the problem, but it's just not possible," Vanessa reiterated. "Now, what other avenues are open to us?"

"I keep thinking of our mission statement, the one you gave me when I first took this job," Gordon said. "Doesn't it state that our task is to provide comprehensive palliative services to the client to the best of our ability, while honoring patient wishes, needs and values? Patients in palliative care often have their pets with them, the things they love around them, the things that comfort them close at hand. I can't see the difference here, except that with Cedric it's a packing box instead of a dog."

Portia wanted to applaud. If she wasn't in love with Nelson, she could certainly fall for this big, stubborn nurse. Vanessa couldn't deny her own mission statement, could she?

"I myself will move Cedric in," Gordon added. "I'll do it with the least possible disruption to the unit. And I'm his primary caregiver, so if there's a problem with any of the nursing procedures, I'll deal with it." He gave Vanessa a steady look. "It's not for long, anyway,'' he reminded her softly, matter-of-factly.

Portia could see Vanessa trying to reconcile her rigid ideas of what was acceptable with her dedication as a caregiver. At last, she grudgingly gave in. "Gordon, I'm holding you responsible for making certain you don't infest the entire unit with vermin," she snapped. "I'm going to have a lot of explaining to do when the nurses see that packing box, so I'd better go prepare them." She stalked out.

"*Yes!*" Portia crowed, shoving an arm in the air in a salute. "Gordon, that was inspired. Congratulations."

He smiled his calm smile. "Now the tough part begins," he said. "Persuading Cedric to move into the Palliative Care Unit might be even harder than convincing Vanessa to have him there."

"Do you want me to come with you to talk to him?" Maybe she could get an intern to cover for her for another hour or so.

Gordon shook his head. "He doesn't mind me knowing where and how he lives, but he'd be embarrassed to have you see it. I'll tell you how it goes."

Portia went back to work, thinking how well Gordon had handled the crisis with Vanessa Thorpe. He'd been explicit in what he wanted, and he'd simply used the basic facts, without becoming distracted by inconsequential details. It was a lesson for her, in how to deal with her mother over Juliet.

The ER was busy all day, but things had slowed down by the time Joanne arrived to begin the evening shift.

"Got a minute?" She pulled Portia into an examining room and closed the door so they wouldn't be overheard. "I went to a seminar a couple months ago that was held by the doctor from Victoria who wrote that book you loaned me a year ago called *Unconditional Healing.*"

"Derek Davis. I remember. He and several other doctors operate the Victoria Pain Clinic." Portia had been intensely interested in the clinic because it was run by medical doctors making use of many alternative treatments, including hypnosis, imagery, massage and spiritual healing.

"Well, I remembered he said at the seminar that he was considering starting a similar clinic here in Vancouver. So I gave him a call this morning, and the clinic's a go. He's now looking for doctors interested in alternative care." Joanne took a card from her pocket and handed it to Portia. "Here's his number. I think he'd be really interested in talking to you. At the seminar he talked about medical intuitives, people who diagnose without even being near the patient, and you came to mind immediately."

Portia studied the card. "It'd be different from working in the ER, that's for sure."

"Change isn't always a bad thing."

"It's sure scary, though." Portia grinned at her friend and stuck the card in the pocket of her trousers. "I'd miss the adrenaline transfusion I get here daily. I'd miss you."

"I don't live here. We could still do lunch. And there're other methods of getting your daily adrenaline rush." Joanne's eyes twinkled. "I'm told sex has a similar effect."

"More fun, too, I've heard." They grinned at each other.

There was a tap at the door, and a nurse stuck her head in. "I have a sixty-year-old female with acute lower abdominal pain in room five. Could one of you have a look?"

"I'll take it, Portia. You go home."

Portia did, and that evening, she phoned her mother. She'd written out her own mission statement before she dialed, and she clutched the paper like a talisman.

A maid answered, and it was a long wait before Lydia finally came on the line, her voice rich and sensual. "Portia, it's almost midnight here. I was having a bath. Malcolm says hello. He wants to know when you're coming down for a holiday. He says he'd like to get better acquainted with you."

"Tell him, me, too." Determined not to get sidetracked, Portia blurted out, "Mom, Juliet's pregnant, and she's planning on keeping her baby."

Silence.

"Mom? I think you should come here so we can make plans. She won't be able to stay in Harmony House once the baby comes. And she's gonna need close supervision after the baby's born—certainly at first, maybe indefinitely."

"There must be someone we can hire. The father is that Stuart person?"

"Stuart Mays, but Juliet's on her own. He's living in Seattle now, and as far as I'm aware, he's staying there."

"Honestly." Lydia blew out an exasperated breath. "I can't just rearrange my life and come to Vancouver right this minute, Portia. Malcolm and I can't get away just now. He's involved in the regatta. And I'd hate to come without him. Besides, I'm working with the police in Amsterdam on a murder case. I'll send a check so you can hire someone—"

Portia reread her mission statement: *My task is to provide support to those I love, but not at the expense of my own happiness, my own life.*

"No, Mother." She remembered how calm Gordon had sounded, and did her best to mimic his tone. "That's what you've always done with Juliet. You send money and expect me to handle the details. But I'm not going to. She's your daughter. It's time you took responsibility for her. She needs you right now.''

"Portia, that's cruel and unfair." Lydia sounded hurt and bewildered. "I've always taken responsibility for all my children, especially for Juliet. Why, she's always had the very best of care. Money's never been an issue, and it isn't now. We simply have to hunt down a good, reliable nanny when the baby comes, and find Juliet a suitable apartment. It's too bad about the group home. I really thought she was settled there permanently.''

"And someone has to take time to do those things,'' she reminded her mother. Portia shut her eyes and shook her head. This was tough. "Besides, those are physical things, Mom. Juliet needs so much more. She loves Stuart, and he's abandoned her. She needs emotional reassurance. She needs to know that you support her in *every* way, not just financially. She needs you here right now, Mom.''

Silence. Then, in a grudging tone, Lydia said, "Well, I'll have to see how I can rearrange my schedule. I'll discuss it with Malcolm and call you back.''

Portia was sweating when she hung up, but she was also pleased with herself. She'd never before been so honest with her mother. Whether Lydia came or not, at least Portia had clearly conveyed what she wanted.

When the phone rang ten minutes later, she snatched it up, wondering what Lydia had decided to do.

"Hi...Mom?"

"Sorry to disappoint you, sweetheart." It was Nelson. "I was thinking of you, so I decided to call."

Hearing his voice, she realized how much she missed him. "How are you, Nelson?" He sounded tense. "How's your mother?"

"I'm at the hospital. Mom's in Intensive Care. I go in to see her for ten minutes out of each hour."

"What do the docs say?"

"They're cautiously optimistic. They feel there's a good chance she'll make a full recovery if she gets through this next twenty-four hours." The tension in his voice increased. "Just sitting around here, not being able to do anything but wait, is damn hard."

"Your mom's aware you're there. That's really important." Knowing what to say was difficult. "Talk to her, Nelson. She'll hear you."

"I do. How're things with you, Portia?"

"Fine. Good, even." She told him about Gordon's campaign to get Cedric's packing box into a room in the Palliative Care Unit. "I dropped by on my way home, and sure enough, Gordon was moving Cedric and all his worldly goods into a room right next to the door. I didn't go in. A couple of Cedric's friends were there helping, and I didn't want to interrupt. I'll see him in the morning. He's got a respiratory infection and the interns are keeping a close eye on him for me.''

"Tell him hi from me. Tell him I'll be by to see him as soon as I get back.''

"Any idea when that'll be?'' She tried her best to keep the question casual.

"No idea just yet. I'll let you know as soon as—'' A woman said something and he answered.

"Sorry, Portia, gotta go. Elaine says Mom's awake and asking for me. I'll call again when I have a minute.''

"I'll be sending you and your mom good thoughts.''

"Thanks, darlin'. Bye.''

He ended the connection abruptly, but Portia hung up more slowly. Wasn't Elaine his first wife's name? Nelson had told her that his mother and his former wife had stayed good friends, and Pennsylvania wasn't that far from Florida. Of course Elaine would be there now.

It took Portia a moment to realize that the emotion she was feeling was jealousy. She was stunned. She had no reason, and no right, to be jealous. Nelson had never given her the slightest indication that there was anything but friendship between Elaine and him now.

Just as he'd never given Portia any indication there was more than body hunger between Portia and him. But knowing all that didn't alter the way she felt.

She wanted to be the one with Nelson right now. She wanted to be the one he turned to when he left the hospital. She wanted to be beside him in his hotel bed, to talk with him, comfort him, hold him and be held by him. The longing was intense and visceral, and scary as hell.

You're in way over your head, Bailey. Get a grip.

CHAPTER THIRTEEN

NELSON CLASPED HIS MOTHER'S hand, rubbing a thumb tenderly over the age spots and protruding veins. After five harrowing days, Madeleine was out of Intensive Care. She'd made an amazing recovery, and now that she felt better, she was desperate to go home. She was being discharged that afternoon; Nelson had arranged for home-nursing care around the clock for as long as her doctor thought it necessary. Nelson understood that Madeleine would relax and improve more quickly in the comfort of her own condo.

He'd be flying home himself in a few more days, as soon as he was certain Madeleine was settled. He was about to tell his mother so, when she turned to him with a sad little smile and said, "Hospitals remind me of your father."

Nelson nodded and a shudder ran down his spine. "Me, too. Hellish memories."

"Some," Madeleine agreed. "But the good far outweigh the bad," she declared. "I'm such a lucky woman to have had the life I had with William."

Her blue eyes, faded replicas of Nelson's own, glowed with an inner light. "We had a wonderful marriage, he and I."

"How can you say that?" The words rushed out of him. "All those years you spent caring for Dad when he wasn't much more than a vegetable, the agony of watching him die a little each day. God, if you'd known about the Huntington's, really known what it would do to him, and to you, you wouldn't have ever—" He stopped, ashamed of his outburst.

"Ever married William?" The blue eyes were searching his face now, and Nelson couldn't meet her steady gaze, but he nodded, and old resentments roiled in his gut.

"You're wrong, son. I understood the chances. Your father never lied to me, not once. He told me all about the disease when we first met," she said. "He even took me to meet his uncle Seth, who already had Huntington's, so I'd see firsthand what it was like. We both realized it was a possibility for William. We spoke of it sometimes, but we vowed to live every moment of every day and take joy in that." She laughed a little. "We did, too. But only after we were married, of course. I used to tease your father about how I'd had to practically use a shotgun to get him to marry me in the first place."

"What do you mean?" Nelson had never asked

questions, never talked to his mother this way, thinking it would upset her. Instead of being upset, she looked almost like a young girl as she recounted how she and William had met at a church social, how she'd pursued him, rather than the other way around.

"He was the most reluctant suitor. He had this idea he couldn't ever marry." Madeleine shook her head. "So of course I had no choice." She met Nelson's eyes and grinned roguishly. "I seduced him. I made sure I got pregnant with you, and that was that. He had to marry me then. It would have been a scandal in those days not to get married. And it was a scandal, anyway. My mother and father were mortified, and furious with both of us. But I knew William was the only man for me, and there was no other way to change his mind."

"You—you got pregnant deliberately?" Nelson was shocked. "Even—even knowing about the Huntington's?" He felt a surge of unreasonable anger at his mother. How could she have done such an irresponsible thing, trapping his father into doing what he'd sworn never to do? Damning her own child with a horrible genetic legacy?

"I've always been an optimist, Nelson. There was as much a chance your father *wouldn't* inherit the disease as there was that he would. I took that chance." A frown came and went. "Some would say I lost, but not me. I had twenty-four marvelous years, filled with laughter and the absolute love of a man I adored. And I have you, my dear boy.'' She looked him straight in the eye. ''I know your father's illness has had a profound effect on your life, and I'm sorry for that. Maybe we made a mistake not telling you about Huntington's from the very beginning. It was such a shock for you when William began to develop the symptoms. And I realize you must worry about developing it. I wish that didn't have to be, and my heart aches for you. But we all have choices, Nelson. We can either live fully each day that we have, or waste our time worrying about dying. We all die eventually, anyway. I pray every day that you're enjoying your life to the fullest and not agonizing about something that may never happen. Are you doing that?''

Her question caught him by surprise. ''I guess I'm doing my best,'' he said after a moment.

''I hope so, dear. Remember that your best today isn't your best tomorrow. We're here to grow. As for doing anything differently myself?'' She shook her head. ''The thought never crosses my mind.''

ON THE PLANE BACK to Vancouver two days later, his mother's words kept echoing in Nelson's head. They'd talked again, and looked at old albums, which had reminded him of the happy times they'd all shared when he was a child, times he'd forgotten when his father's illness had taken precedence.

He could understand Madeleine's point of view now, even if he couldn't completely share it. And he'd renewed a bond with her that he'd done his best to break. He'd call her when he got home. It was good to have his mother back in his life.

He glanced at his watch, impatient for the long plane ride to be over. He'd already phoned Portia; she was meeting him at the Vancouver terminal.

He couldn't wait to hold her in his arms, hear her voice, her laughter. He couldn't wait to make love to her. He'd done a great deal of thinking, and at some point during the past forty-eight hours, he'd admitted that he'd fallen in love with Portia. It had taken a huge amount of courage to admit, even to himself, that he wanted to marry her.

He didn't just want it—he longed for it. He fantasized how it would be, he and Portia, committed to each other, living under the same roof, making the concessions that married people make. Anxiety ate at his guts, though, each time he tried to figure out how she felt about him.

She enjoyed their lovemaking; he had no doubts in that quarter. She enjoyed talking with him; they never ran out of things to say. They'd been together through some tough times—his injuries, Juliet's pregnancy. Getting through bad times together should mean that good times would be a snap.

But did she love him? The only way to find out was to ask her. He'd get a ring, he decided. He'd do the whole thing right.

He didn't have his mother's fatalistic courage, however.

Before he could ask the woman he loved to be his partner, he would have to find out once and for all whether he had Huntington's.

Within the next couple of days, he'd call the genetics laboratory at the University of British Columbia and ask for the test.

And when the answer came, then he'd know what to say to Portia.

"YOU LOOK SO *GOOD*," he told her. "Damn, you are one good-looking woman, Dr. Bailey."

She laughed. She'd been standing at the front of the crowd, just outside the door he came through when he cleared Customs, and hers was the first and only face he saw.

He'd thought he remembered exactly how she looked, but he'd forgotten how the dramatic angularity of her jaw contrasted with the soft vulnerability of her mouth. He'd forgotten how her gray eyes reflected the smile on her lips. He'd forgotten how those lips tasted when he kissed her, how his

hand fit in the small of her back and her slender
body tilted against him, pliable and willing, when
he drew her close.

"Let's get out of here." His voice was harsh, and
he wished he didn't have the damn crutches so he
could have wrapped one arm around her neck and
looped his raincoat over the other to hide the erection that wouldn't subside as they walked through
the terminal, out to the parking garage.

He shoved his luggage in the trunk of the Datsun,
and before she could get in the car, he leaned the
crutches against the door and took her in his arms
again, as hungry for her as if she were oxygen.

"I missed you more than I can say," he whispered, running his palm over her short, spiky hair,
surprised as always that instead of being bristly, it
was soft, like feathers beneath his fingers. "I want
you so bad I can barely walk or put two coherent
sentences together."

"Wow. You'll have to go away again if coming
back makes you like this," she murmured, and he
felt the warm brush of her breath against his neck.

"I suppose there's some dumb law against making love right here in the airport garage," he said.

She pretended to look around. "I don't see any
signs posted, but just from a practical standpoint,
my car's too cramped and the cement's hard and

cold. Get in. We'll go to my place. I'm making you dinner, and the sheets are clean.''

"I thought you didn't cook."

"Stir-fry. I make a mean stir-fry."

He'd been to her house before, but this time it seemed different. The table was set, candles glowed, soft music played. Suddenly it felt like home to him. "If I didn't know better, Doc, I'd think you were trying to seduce me. Is there wine to go with all this?''

She gave him a look that set his blood on fire. "I think maybe some of my psychic powers are rubbing off on you. The bottle's in the fridge.''

"Good place for it. Will the stir-fry keep?"

"Absolutely."

"Can I have a peek at those clean sheets?"

She smiled at him, a lazy, feline smile. "Follow me, sir. You'll be impressed.''

HIS BREATHING SLOWED. Her breasts were against his chest; a knee rested on his thigh. Her head was tucked into the curve of his shoulder.

Sex and love. He understood the connection now. All that poetry made perfect sense…all those rhyming words about two being one. It wasn't poetry; it was fact. They were one organism, he and she.

She took his hand and threaded her fingers through his.

"Talk to me, Nelson. What's bothering you?"

She propped herself up on an elbow and gave him the half-unfocused look he'd come to recognize. "There're a lot of red ripples around you, strong feelings of some kind. What's going on?"

"I'm in love with you, Portia." He hadn't intended to tell her yet, but now that he'd said the words, he felt intense relief. "I realized it on the plane coming home."

Her gray eyes widened and her smile lit up her face. "Well, that's good to hear, because I'm in love with you, too."

"You are? In love with me?" Elation filled him, but it was quickly tempered by what had to happen before he could take things any further. "I'm going for the genetic testing, Portia...as soon as I can get in. And until I have the results, I can't promise you anything."

Her eyes, the misty gray of spring rain, were steady on his face. "You mean like marriage and happily ever after."

Her tone sounded kind of flat. He couldn't tell what it meant. "Yeah. Something like that." He thought of his mother getting pregnant so his dad would marry her. He couldn't do anything like that. "I have to be certain I have a future before we start planning on it."

"I've told you before and I'm telling you now that you don't have the damn disease." Now he could hear the impatience in her voice. "I can't tell whether you'll ever get it, but I can't guarantee, either, that I'm not going to have a heart attack or die of cancer in the next ten years.'' Now her voice was low and intense. ''It really pisses me off that you don't trust me, Nelson.''

He opened his mouth to assure her that he did, but closed it again. On this particular subject, he couldn't afford to trust something as nebulous as psychic ability. ''You tell me I don't have it now, Portia, but before I involve you in my life, I've got to know once and for all whether I'm carrying the gene.''

She punched the pillow hard, inches from his head, and he jumped. ''You're such a stubborn, idiotic fool at times. I'm already involved in your life. I've just told you I love you. How much more involved can I get?''

There was danger here. Her very involvement was what troubled him. ''If I've got it, I'll have to leave, Portia.'' Voicing what he'd decided made it real, and he could feel the sickening yank in his guts that said he wouldn't want to go on living without the woman next to him. The stakes had changed; it wasn't getting Huntington's that was now his worst fear. It was losing Portia.

She was crouched on the bed now, staring at him. ''So you'll walk out if the test results are positive? You'll leave me because of something that won't even happen for years and years?'' Her voice rose, and he could see the anger in her eyes, the tension in every line of her beautiful naked body.

"You'll just put me on hold and wait for some scientific test to determine how we spend the rest of our lives?"

She was trembling. He reached out a hand to smooth her arm and she knocked it away.

"You don't get it, Nelson. This *is* my life, right here, right now."

"You're the one who doesn't get it." His anger at the disease, at himself, at what was happening between them, made him lose control. He was shouting at her. "I'm trying to protect you. What the hell's wrong with that? I don't intend to ever be your patient, Portia. I want to be your husband, your lover. When I know I have time, then we'll take the next step. Until then—"

She was out of bed in a flash and pulling on her clothes. "Forget *until then*. Get out, Nelson. Now. I don't feel like living in a vacuum for the next six or eight weeks or however long it takes. I'd rather be alone than on probation." She was gone before he could think of anything to say.

It took him twenty minutes to dress and call a cab. Although he looked for Portia in every corner of the house, she was nowhere to be found.

THE FOLLOWING MORNING in the genetics department at the University of British Columbia, Nelson sat across from a rumpled, grandmotherly woman in a white smock and tried to dissociate himself as she wrapped a rubber tube around his arm and withdrew a vial of blood. His heart was hammering, and he felt as if he were stepping off a cliff. He stared at the blood in the tube. Would it give him the gift of time or rob him of it?

"It'll be thirty-four days before we have the result," she reminded him. "Try to stay optimistic, Mr. Gregory." Her faded blue eyes were kind and caring. "Remember that out of every four hundred tests we do, only one hundred and fifty are positive. The odds are on your side."

Thirty-four days. Thirty-four nights.

He'd tried to call Portia last night and again this morning, but she wasn't answering, which probably was for the best, because he couldn't apologize for or change anything he'd said. All he could do now was wait. Unless he occupied his mind and his body, he'd go mad.

He saw a public telephone far down the hallway and hurried toward it, pausing only to dig the phone number for the flight school out of his wallet.

CHAPTER FOURTEEN

"AREN'T YOU HUNGRY, JULES?" Portia eyed the plate of pancakes and eggs she'd placed in front of her sister. Juliet had asked her for this particular breakfast, but after Portia had gone to all the trouble of fixing it, Juliet hadn't eaten more than two bites.

"The baby makes me feel full all the time." Juliet toyed with the syrup container, snapping the lid open and closed, open and closed. It got on Portia's nerves, as most things did these days. Eleven days had passed since the fight with Nelson; she ought to be getting over the black funk she'd been in. How long did it take a broken heart to heal?

"I liked Dr. Jacobsen, Portia. But I don't like to pee in that little cup. It goes all over my hands and I don't like that. I don't want to do that again, Portia."

The previous afternoon, Portia had accompanied Juliet on her first visit to the obstetrician. Morgan had taken infinite pains to reassure Juliet, but Jules had still been apprehensive and nervous, so much so that Morgan had performed only the most basic of tests, confirming that Juliet was pregnant. She'd wanted to do blood tests, but Juliet had thrown such a fuss at the sight of the needle, Morgan postponed it.

"I have a hunch she could be further along than we think," Morgan had told Portia while Juliet was dressing. "I'm going to my daughter's wedding in New Hampshire next week. I'll schedule an ultrasound the moment I get back. And we'll have to take blood then, no matter how upset she becomes."

"I'll prepare her as best I can," Portia said, sighing.

Juliet's pregnancy was going to tax them all to their limits.

Juliet snapped the lid, up, down.

"Stop fooling with the syrup and go get dressed," Portia ordered. "We've got to pick up Mother in less than an hour." At least Lydia had made the decision to come to Vancouver. She was flying in this morning.

"I am dressed already." Juliet was wearing worn green track pants and a purple top with Barbie stenciled across the front.

"You know how Mom is about clothes, Jules. She wants you to look nice. She's invited us for lunch at the hotel. It'll be fancy."

Juliet's face took on a rebellious cast. "So that's not my problem, right?" This was Juliet's latest catchphrase. "She's gonna be mad at me, anyway. It won't matter what I wear."

Portia didn't have the energy to argue. Besides, there was some truth to it. "Okay, get your coat and let's go."

Juliet didn't move.

"Are you sick again, Jules?"

She shook her head. "Not in the morning anymore, but I was last night, remember?" She twisted on the chair, shrugging her shoulders and moving her head from side to side. "I got a crick in my shoulder. It's sore, Portia. Can I take an aspirin or something? 'Cause it really, really hurts me."

"Sure, an aspirin won't do any harm. You probably slept the wrong way." Juliet had complained about fifty different ailments since the previous evening. Her legs ached, her head hurt, her stomach was sore, her breasts were tender. She'd even said her heart hurt, a complaint that Portia could sympathize with, because it felt as if her own was breaking in two.

Portia found an aspirin, got Juliet into her coat, and at last they were on their way.

Being at the airport reminded Portia of the excitement and joy she'd felt just days ago when she'd picked Nelson up, and as she walked with Juliet to the international arrivals level, she felt a wave of such utter despair she could hardly bear it.

"There's our mother. Hey, Mother." Juliet, excited now, waved both arms over her head. "Mama, Mom, we're here, see?"

Lydia swept through the doors wheeling a luggage cart with three immense suitcases. She hugged her daughters, but before Portia located the car in the parking garage, Lydia was making it plain she was put out with both of them.

"Juliet, I'm so disappointed in you. I thought you had more sense than to go and get pregnant," she chided as Portia heaved the suitcases in the trunk. "I thought Portia made sure you knew about birth control."

"I do know. Portia told me and told me. But I *wanted* to have a baby with Stuart." Juliet's voice rose, and people nearby turned to stare.

It was obvious to Portia that tears and a tantrum were imminent.

"Get in the car, Jules. We can talk inside just as well as out here," she urged.

Juliet got in the back and slammed the door. "I love Stuart. And I don't care that you're mad at me, Mother. It's my life. It's my baby. If you're mad, that's not my problem, right?"

Portia heard her mother's intake of breath. This was going to get disastrous in just one more minute, and she was in no mood for it.

"Stop, both of you." Her tone was sharp, her

voice loud, and her surprised family paid attention. "We'll discuss everything, but not right now. I have to drive through pouring rain and heavy traffic, and I'm not doing it with you two arguing all the way. When we get to the hotel, we'll discuss what's going to be best for you, Juliet. And the baby." *And me.*

"Well, I would have thought you could do that without dragging me all the way up here in the middle of the winter, Portia." Lydia shivered and drew her elegant sheepskin-lined raincoat tighter around her.

Portia bit her tongue, turned up the heat and concentrated on driving. Her passengers were silent as she swept over the bridge, down Granville Street and over another bridge to the downtown core.

She'd invited Lydia to stay at the house, but her mother preferred the luxury of a hotel, and Portia told herself she was relieved. Having fastidious Lydia as a houseguest would have given her hives, anyway.

As it was, she longed to drop Lydia and Juliet under the portico of the waterfront hotel and just drive away. For a moment, she considered it, but a glimpse of her sister's woebegone face in the rearview mirror convinced her that she had to stay, for Juliet's sake.

But she wouldn't allow Lydia to shove all the

responsibility for Juliet's care on her, Portia vowed. As childish as it had seemed, she'd stuck her mission statement in the pocket of her slacks, and she would stay focused on it, no matter what Lydia said or didn't say. Portia would provide support for Juliet, but not at the cost of her own life or happiness.

Happiness? Portia handed the car keys to the hotel valet and followed Lydia and Juliet into the opulent lobby. Happiness was a joke. She'd fired the man she loved, who'd told her he loved her. She wanted him to trust her instincts, take her word that he didn't have Huntington's, while she was expending huge amounts of energy at St. Joe's to keep from using those very instincts. How much more rational could she be?

Nelson, her job, her family—everything about her life was making her feel exhausted and frustrated. Whatever this horrible mix of emotions inside her was, Portia was clear about one thing: this wasn't happiness.

They went up to the suite of rooms and waited for the bellboy to bring the suitcases. Lydia suggested going down again to the dining room for lunch, then blanched when she saw what Juliet was wearing under her coat. She hastily ordered them a room service meal.

When it came, Portia picked at her salad, and she noticed that Juliet barely touched the fries and gravy she'd requested. Lydia was the only one who devoured her own salad with honest hunger.

"Can I lie down on the bed in there?" Juliet pointed at the bedroom. "I'm really, really sleepy. I need to lie down. Dr. Jacobsen said if I was tired I should just sleep."

Portia could see that her mother was relieved when Juliet curled up under the duvet. A few moments later the sound of her soft snores came from the bedroom.

"So, what are we going to do about her?" Lydia held her china teacup to her lips and sipped.

"We're going to wait till Juliet wakes up, and then you're going to discuss things with her. She has pretty clear-cut ideas of her own."

Lydia set the cup down, alarm on her patrician features. "But surely you have some suggestions, Portia. You know that I don't always understand Juliet."

"You'll learn." Feeling this irritable made her say things she normally would only have thought.

Lydia gave Portia a long, considering look, as though she was seeing her for the first time since she'd arrived. "What's the matter with you, Portia? You're not usually like this."

Portia shrugged. "I'm just saying what I think."

Lydia was still studying her. "You're thinner than when I saw you last year. It's becoming, but watch that you don't go too far. Your face could easily start to appear haggard instead of dramatic. Not that I've ever had that problem. I've gained seven pounds since Malcolm and I were married, all on my butt." Lydia patted her ample behind. "Malcolm swears he likes it, but I certainly don't."

"Are you happy, Mom?" Damn. Now, why had that popped out? This happy thing was really getting under Portia's skin. "I don't mean about the weight or with Malcolm. I just mean generally. Happy. Are you?"

To Portia's surprise, Lydia took the question seriously. "I think so, yes. Mostly. A lot more often than when I was younger. Everyone has lapses when it comes to being really happy. Anyway, *you* don't have to ask, do you? I'm sure you can tell by seeing me. A person's aura is a perfect barometer when it comes to the truth."

"I'm trying not to see auras."

"Oh? And why is that?"

Cursing herself for even bringing up the subject, Portia explained about Betty Hegard. "I was formally chastised by the hospital board and warned not to do anything like that again."

"Fools," Lydia snorted. "Surely you aren't going to let that bother you. It's only fear, you know, and ignorance. People are afraid of what they don't understand. Heavens, I still get called a witch in some newspaper articles.''

''Did you ever want to stop using your ability?''

''Of course. I still do occasionally.'' Lydia poured more tea into her cup and nibbled at a chocolate éclair. ''It's not the most pleasant thing, seeing where bodies are hidden, feeling what happened to them, sensing the terror of people, sometimes even their death. I saw a movie a while ago about a boy who saw dead people. It was very accurate. I was like that boy when I was young. I didn't tell anyone about the things I saw, either.''

''Not even Grandma?'' Portia's grandmother had been able to foresee the future.

''Of course I told Mother. She understood. But she wasn't altogether happy that I'd inherited the family's psychic streak. She didn't want me to be different, the way she'd been all her life. She wanted me to be normal—be a cheerleader and go to the prom with the captain of the football team.''

Lydia giggled. ''So I did. His name was Allen Suefeld, and when Mother met him, she told me not to have anything more to do with him, that he was going to come to a bad end. She was right, of course. He embezzled money and landed in jail.''

''Did she ever tell you what my life was going to be like?'' Her grandma had died when Portia was only eight. Right now she'd give anything to have someone say she would fall in love with a handsome man, get married and live happily ever after. But then, she'd already done the love - and - the - handsome - man bit. It was the happily ever after that eluded her.

Lydia shook her head. "The only thing she ever said was that you'd be a healer. She didn't like to predict when it came to her own family." Lydia swallowed the last of the éclair. "Now, who's this man you're in love with, dear?"

"What?" Portia was taken aback.

"You *are* in love, aren't you? I thought so when I first saw you. It makes some women lose weight, and if things aren't going well, it can certainly make you cranky. And you *are* cranky and thin. So who is he?"

"He—his name's Nelson Gregory." The words came haltingly at first, but once she'd begun, she couldn't seem to stop. She told Lydia about the Huntington's, about Nelson's refusal to trust her intuition about the disease, his refusal to make any plans until the test came back.

"Well, that doesn't surprise me, Portia," Lydia remarked. "Why should he trust you when you don't trust yourself?"

Indignation made her bristle. "That's a rotten thing to say." Why had she ever confided in Lydia?

She should have known better. Her mother had never been supportive.

"But it's true, isn't it? You told me you've stopped trying to see. And we both know that unless you use your ability, you lose it. Which is fine if that's really what you want. But I've always felt we have it for a reason, even if we don't know what that reason is. And I think letting a bunch of doctors or whoever they are bully you into submission isn't healthy."

Juliet came wandering out of the bedroom just then, rubbing her eyes and yawning. Portia was grateful for the interruption. She didn't need any more of her mother's advice. She felt more irritable than ever, and anxious. She wanted to get the issues with Juliet settled so that she could go home and be by herself.

"I had this dream," Juliet announced. "It was the best dream. Stuart and I were getting married. I had this pretty dress and a lace thing on my head, and I wanted the dream to go on and on. I hated waking up. Portia, my shoulder still hurts and I'm really, really thirsty. Can I have some juice?"

Lydia ordered it. For the next half hour, Portia did her best to help her sister verbalize her sadness about Stuart and her joy over the baby. Lydia made an effort to listen; Portia had to credit her with that.

It gave her an idea. She stood up and retrieved her coat from the closet.

"Are we going already?" Juliet got to her feet.

"Not you, Jules. I'm going. You're staying here with Mom. The two of you have stuff to talk about, private stuff."

Portia saw the alarm on her mother's face, the uncertainty on Juliet's, and she had a pang of guilt at abandoning them, but she subdued it. If mother and daughter were ever going to reach a point where they were comfortable with each other, it had to happen without Portia running interference.

"I have to work tomorrow, so Mom will see that you get back to Harmony House tonight, Jules."

"How?" Juliet's chin was wobbling.

"In a taxi." Portia went over and hugged her sister. Juliet clung to her, and as she held her, Portia felt a stab of alarm. Juliet, too, had lost weight in the past few weeks. She felt fragile. But there was something else, as well, something that Portia had been too self-absorbed, too distracted, too bad-tempered, to notice till now.

Portia stepped back and really looked at her sister, willing herself to see the colors she'd been doing her best to ignore, and what she saw sent raw fear coursing through her veins.

"Juliet, when do you see Dr. Jacobsen again?"

"You know, the nurse wrote it down on that little

card, not next week, the week after. You remember. Dr. Jacobsen's going away because her daughter's getting married. She's gonna wear a white dress and I wish I could get married like in my dream, Portia. Don't go and leave me here, okay?''

Portia wasn't listening. ''We need to get you to the hospital, Jules. Right now.''

CHAPTER FIFTEEN

LYDIA LOOKED SHOCKED, and Juliet began whining.

"But just my shoulder hurts, Portia. I can have an aspirin. Remember you said—"

Portia was bundling Juliet into her coat. Juliet resisted.

"I don't wanna go to the hospital. They give you needles there. I don't like needles. I don't want to. I don't like it there. Why do I have to?"

"What's going on, Portia? What do you see?" Lydia spoke quietly, but her face reflected her concern.

"This pregnancy is ectopic. The fallopian tube is in danger of bursting. We need to go to St. Joe's right now."

The urgency in her voice was enough to convince Lydia. She threw her coat on and called down to make certain Portia's car would be waiting.

Juliet wailed and resisted. It took both Lydia and Portia to put her in the car, and within moments they were on their way.

Portia tried to calm Juliet, but her sister was beyond reason. She howled the entire short distance, and when Portia wheeled into St. Joe's emergency entrance, Juliet was hysterical. Portia needed the help of two orderlies to get Juliet out of the car and into a wheelchair.

Once inside, Portia ordered a sedative. Examining room three was empty, and Portia wheeled her sister in.

As soon as the drug took effect, Juliet quieted and listened. Lydia, too, paid attention as Portia explained what was wrong and what had to be done.

She used a diagram of an egg and a sperm, and a chart of a woman's body. "This is the uterus, where a baby grows. But sometimes the fertilized egg doesn't go to the right place. That's what's happened with you, Jules." She pointed to the fallopian tubes. "Your pregnancy is implanted here, and it's very dangerous." She drew a deep breath, because she knew Juliet was going to be devastated when she finally understood. "We have to stop it from growing more, Jules. If we leave it there, you could die. You could bleed into the abdominal cavity...here."

"So you can just move it, right? You can move my baby to the right place. Can't you, Portia?"

The trust her sister had in her was heartbreaking.

"No, Juliet." Why did things have to be so difficult? "There's no way anyone can do that." She said what had to be said. "There's not going to be a baby, honey." Not this time. Maybe not ever, if the fallopian tube had to be removed and there was any sort of problem with the other one.

Portia tried to curb her sense of urgency, not wanting to frighten Lydia or Juliet more than necessary. "If possible, we'll only remove the embryo. But if the likelihood of rupture is high, we may have to take the tube out. First we're going to do an ultrasound. It's a test where a radiologist looks at a screen and sees what's inside your tummy, Jules. It won't hurt, I promise. I'll come along and hold your hand the whole while."

Juliet began to cry, the openmouthed wails that Portia was used to but that had always embarrassed Lydia. Now, however, she wrapped her arms around Juliet and held her, crooning comfort.

Juliet wouldn't be comforted, however. "I want Stuart. I love Stuart. It's his baby, too. Make him come here, Portia. I want him here with me. Please get him to come here, Mama." She sniffled. "I'm scared."

Lydia glanced at Portia and then used a tissue on Juliet's cheeks and nose. "I'll try to find him, honey. Do you have a phone number for him?"

Juliet dug a dog-eared paper from her purse. "This is his sister's number. Her name is Bernice. But she'll be mad if you tell her it's about me. His mother told Bernice not to let me talk to Stuart. His mother doesn't like me. She says I'm a slut."

"She does, does she?" Lydia's eyes flashed fire. She pursed her lips and snatched the paper. "You go with Portia now, and I'll do my best to get Stuart here."

"You promise? You promise, Mama?"

"I promise." Lydia marched off in search of a telephone.

For Portia, the next few hours were filled with decisions. The blood tests and ultrasound confirmed what she'd intuitively known.

Juliet had an ectopic pregnancy, and just as Morgan had thought, the fetus was further developed than suspected. The fallopian tube was dangerously enlarged, on the verge of rupture. That negated the possibility of using the drug methotrexate, which destroyed a pregnancy by halting cell growth. Immediate surgery was necessary. Juliet's life could be in danger.

And once again, Portia could tell from the questions her co-workers asked and the sidelong glances they gave her that everyone was speculating on how she could possibly have known the danger Juliet was in. The admitting history showed no symptoms apart from the sore shoulder Juliet had complained of that morning. There had been no bleeding, no pain, no visible motive for rushing her into Emerg and ordering tests.

As she'd always done, Portia simply said she'd had a hunch something was not right.

Lydia was gone for some time. When she returned, Juliet was already prepped for surgery. She'd been given tranquilizing drugs, but still she tried to sit up when her mother appeared beside the stretcher.

"Is Stuart coming to see me, Mama?" Her voice was thick, her eyelids heavy. "Is he coming? I *need* Stuart. I *need* him."

"I'm sorry, honey. I couldn't find him." Lydia's jaw was set, and she looked as if she'd been doing battle. "I tried my best, but really, those relatives of his are not helpful in the least. He's not living with his sister anymore. He moved out two days ago. I finally pried out of Bernice the name of the car dealership where Stuart's been working, likely illegally. But the man who answered said that Stuart only worked mornings. He didn't have a phone number or an address for wherever Stuart is presently living."

"Stuart's not coming? He's not coming to see me?" Juliet's voice was agonized, and she started to cry again.

"I'll keep trying to get hold of him," Lydia assured her. "I'll find a way to get him here, even if I have to go and bring him myself."

"Promise, Mama. Promise you'll go and bring him."

"Mother can't promise that, Jules. All we can promise is we'll do our very best." Portia stroked her sister's hair and eased her back down on the stretcher.

"Time to go, young lady." An orderly came to wheel Juliet into the OR. When she was gone, Portia turned to her mother.

"One of us will have to go to Seattle and track him down. That's all there is to it. Did his sister say why he'd moved out?"

Lydia shook her head. "No. And she was very defensive. She wouldn't give me any information, except that he was working at that car dealership...washing cars. The man I spoke to there was very friendly. He said Stuart was a hard worker and reliable. He also said he didn't know Stuart's new address, but he's living with someone named Edgar. The manager would know, but he, too, had left for the day." She handed Portia a scrap of paper with numbers and names scribbled across it. "I'd be quite willing to fly down and try to locate Stuart, but I called the airport and there aren't any seats available until tomorrow afternoon. How I'll ever convince him to come back with me, I don't know. I've never met him.''

Since Lydia had never connected with Juliet, it was unlikely that she'd develop any sort of immediate rapport with Stuart, even if she did manage to locate him. Seattle was a big city. And Stuart wasn't going to trust a stranger.

There was only one solution. Portia's heart sank, and now her mission statement seemed like a mockery. "I'll drive down and see if I can find him," she sighed. "But I don't want to leave until Juliet's out of surgery."

Portia had no objectivity whatsoever when it was her sister undergoing surgery. Her usual composure had totally deserted her by the time the surgeon, Dr. James Burke, came in to say that the operation was over.

"I'm afraid the fallopian tube was irreparably damaged and had to be removed," Burke reported. "Unfortunately, the other tube is not fully developed, which means that it won't be possible for Juliet to become pregnant again, at least not in the normal fashion.''

Tears welled up in Portia's eyes, and for a moment she couldn't respond. Juliet's baby would have posed an enormous problem, requiring all manner of support. But the loss of the baby—and the realization, as well, that she'd never have another— would bring Juliet terrible sadness.

Finding Stuart was even more urgent now. Juliet would need all the support and love available when she learned the news.

Burke left, and Lydia reached out and took Portia's hand. It was an unprecedented gesture on her mother's part; Lydia had never been demonstrative. "It's going to be tough to explain this to her, isn't it?"

Portia nodded. "Yeah. She'll be waking up soon, and she'll want Stuart. I'll just have to go to Seattle and see what I can do."

"How long's the drive from Vancouver?"

"Three hours, depending on the traffic at the border." Another hour or two to locate Stuart. Three hours back. She'd be lucky to get in on time for work tomorrow morning. She'd have to ask if someone could take her shift.

The prospect of the long drive and sleepless night was daunting, but Portia could see no alternative.

They went up to Recovery. Juliet was doing well, the nurse reported, but she was still far too groggy from the anesthesia to hold a conversation. She opened her eyes when Portia spoke to her but fell instantly asleep again.

She'd be moved to the surgical floor within the

hour, and by then Portia hoped she'd be more responsive.

"Let's have something to eat, and then I'll leave," she suggested to Lydia. She felt exhausted, and she hoped that at least part of that was hunger.

They'd just sat down with their trays in the cafeteria when Gordon Caldwell came in. When he was finished making his selections, Portia waved him over to their table. "Care to join us?"

She introduced him to Lydia and explained to her mother that Gordon was the caregiver for one of her favorite patients.

"What a coincidence to find you here. I just called your home number," Gordon said. "Cedric wanted to see you this evening. He wanted me to get hold of you and ask if you'd stop by."

"I took the day off. I planned to see him tomorrow morning first thing."

Portia was in the habit of popping into the Palliative Care Unit to visit Cedric three or four times each day. He'd had a difficult few days settling in, but once he realized that Portia and his street friends would come and visit and that the hospital staff were there to make him comfortable and not lecture him about his packing crate, he'd relaxed. Sadly, his condition continued to deteriorate rapidly.

"He's getting morphine every couple of hours," Gordon said.

Portia understood that Gordon was telling her Cedric's pain had increased dramatically—the progression from Tylenol 3 to morphine had been recent, and the increase in the dosage was significant.

"It's getting harder for him to talk. There was a big change just this afternoon. I'm spending as much time as I can with him," Gordon said.

Again, Gordon and Portia exchanged meaningful glances. They both realized Cedric didn't have much longer to live. If he'd been asking for her, Portia knew she had to go to him immediately. She gulped her sandwich, excused herself and left her mother and Gordon discussing the fishing in Bermuda.

Cedric's room was large and bright, with windows that looked out on a small grassy courtyard. The rough wooden packing crate Gordon had collapsed and reconstructed inside the room took up most of the space, leaving just enough for Cedric to maneuver his wheelchair in and out of the bathroom.

"Knock, knock." Portia waited outside the crate until Cedric responded.

"Doc." His voice was noticeably weaker than it had been just the day before, but the smile he gave Portia was wide and welcoming. His words were little more than a gasp, the drawl almost unintelligible, and there was no poetry to greet her, as there usually was.

Portia bent her head as she came through the low doorway.

Inside the crate, the old mattress he'd slept on had been replaced by a narrow, high-tech hospital bed, but it was covered with Cedric's worn green sleeping bag. In the corners of the crate, stacked cardboard cartons held his beloved books. His few items of clothing as well as his combination tape player and radio were on a folding table. Gordon had asked if he wanted a television, but Cedric had refused.

Portia was used to perching on the bed during her visits. She did so, hiding the shock she felt at the dramatic change in Cedric's appearance in the few hours since she'd last seen him. He seemed to have shrunk. Only the light in his luminous eyes was the same. She took his hand in hers, stroking skin stretched tight over birdlike bones.

"How's it going, my friend?"

"Can't—talk," he whispered.

"That's okay. I'll talk for both of us. Do you need more painkiller?"

He made a tiny negative movement with his head and tried to smile.

To amuse him, Portia had fallen into the habit of telling him anecdotes about her life, turning it into the soap opera Joanne had once teased her about. She'd told Cedric about her psychic ability and the problems it had caused. At first, she'd avoided talking about Nelson, believing that Cedric would be hurt if she confessed her love for another man.

But he'd known without her saying a word. He'd asked her point-blank if she and Nelson were going to get married. She'd said no and changed the subject.

She told him now about Juliet, relieving him of the effort it took to speak. She was explaining what an ectopic pregnancy was when Nelson's voice sounded outside the packing crate.

"Anybody home? Can I come in?"

Portia froze. She hadn't seen Nelson since the night she'd asked him to leave her house, and she didn't want to see him now. She knew he was in the habit of visiting Cedric regularly—Gordon had told her he stopped by most evenings—and she'd always managed to avoid meeting him here.

She couldn't just get up and leave; she'd hardly spent five minutes with Cedric. Her heart began racing, and she could feel nervous perspiration trickle between her breasts.

Cedric's features registered an eager welcome, and Portia could see by the expression on Nelson's face when he came through the low doorway and saw her that he was as shocked by and unprepared for this meeting as she was.

Worst of all, in the cramped space there was nowhere for him to sit. He stood a few inches away, leaning on a cane. She could feel his warmth, smell his familiar scent, even catch a whiff of coffee on his breath.

"Hello, Portia." She caught the strain in his voice, but he smiled at her before he turned to Cedric.

"I was glad Gordon called, because I'd just picked up the photos I took on my last training flight," he said. He tipped them out of an envelope and held them up for Cedric, describing each one in vivid detail.

Portia barely listened. Instead, she was remembering how it felt to be in Nelson's arms, to laugh with him, to lie beside him at night. How his skin smelled and tasted. How the furry pelt on his chest felt soft to her palm. How he snored when he lay on his back and how he reached for her the moment he awoke. And she couldn't deny the gaping hole inside her chest where her heart should be.

How laughable that she'd thought, even for an instant, that she might be getting over him. She loved him as much as ever, and to know that it was over between them hurt worse than anything she'd ever experienced.

"Juliet's in the hospital," Portia said to fill in the silence when Nelson finished with the pictures. "She had to have an operation."

"What happened?" Nelson's eyes filled with concern, and she explained once again, her voice thick, about the ectopic pregnancy.

"Is Stuart aware? I'll bet Juliet wants him with her."

"She does." Portia was touched at how well he'd come to understand her sister. "My mother's here at St. Joe's with Juliet. I'm driving to Seattle to see if Stuart will come back with me."

"When are you leaving?"

"Right away."

"Why not let me arrange for a flight, instead?" Nelson's offer was immediate. "A friend from the flight school has a private jet. It would be lots faster. I'll go with you."

Portia began to shake her head, but Nelson persisted.

"Look, it's nearly dark out and it's raining hard," he reminded her. "Driving will take hours. The jet would get us there in forty minutes, tops. I'll have a car waiting, and I'm familiar with Seattle. We can pick up Stuart and be back here before Juliet's fully awake."

Portia longed to refuse. The last thing she wanted today was to spend time with Nelson. It would be just too emotionally draining. But what he said made sense. She didn't know Seattle at all, and driving there and back was scary. She'd never been much good with maps.

Cedric had been paying close attention. He caught Portia's eye and tried to nod. He was obviously encouraging her to accept.

In deference to Cedric, Portia dug the paper her mother had scribbled on out of her pocket and handed it to Nelson. In doing so, she knew she was accepting the help he was offering.

"I'll line up the flight," Nelson said. "I'll be right outside." With a promise to Cedric that he'd visit soon, Nelson left.

"Go." Cedric's faint voice had an urgency.

Portia smiled at him and caught a glimpse of his aura. A shiver ran down her spine. The aura was fading, disappearing.

"Cedric," she blurted. "I can't leave you, not like this, not now."

He smiled at her. "Gordon's...coming."

She felt torn and raw, stretched paper thin by the conflicting demands of those she loved. She should stay with Cedric. She needed to go for Stuart. She didn't want to be alone with Nelson. She'd promised Juliet.

"Go," Cedric breathed again, and she realized she had no real choice, but still she hesitated. On impulse, she bent and kissed Cedric on the lips. "Good night, my dear friend. I'll come and see you the moment I get back, no matter what time it is."

He moved his head just a little in a nod, and the effort it took to speak brought sweat to his forehead. "'Adieu, adieu, and yet again, adieu,'" he quoted, and tears glimmered in his beautiful eyes.

CHAPTER SIXTEEN

NELSON WAS WAITING OUTSIDE, as he'd said.

"By the time we get to the airport, the plane will be fueled and ready for us." Without touching her, he walked beside Portia toward Emergency, where she'd abandoned her car.

"You're barely limping at all. You're not even on crutches anymore."

"The last of the casts came off two days ago."

"Congratulations." There was something else she had to say to him, and it was difficult. "I'm very grateful for your help, Nelson. But—"

"But it doesn't change anything between us," he interrupted. "I'm aware of that." His voice was steady, reassuring. They'd reached the car and he held out a hand and gave her a lopsided smile. "We're just friends, Portia, I know that."

Her insides felt as if they were collapsing, but she mustered a smile in return and took his hand. "Friends," she agreed through the thickness in her throat. "Thanks, Nelson."

Friends, bullshit. Just the touch of her hand was

enough to set him off, and he had to remind himself that nothing had changed. There were still twenty-three days to live through before he'd know whether he even had a future to look forward to. but it took every ounce of willpower to restrain the urge to drag her into his arms and kiss her senseless.

He held the car door and she climbed in behind the wheel. As he got in beside her, his cell phone was ringing, and for the rest of the ride to the airport he was busy trying to track down someone who knew where Stuart Mays was living. He was grateful to be busy. It kept his hands from wandering to Portia.

By the time they were airborne, he had an address for Stuart. During the short flight they talked about Cedric and Juliet and his mother, and in the silences he tried not to look at Portia.

It seemed only moments from the time they took off until they were coming in for a landing. It was raining in Seattle, although not as hard as it had been in Vancouver.

The car he'd ordered was waiting, and after he'd spoken with the pilot about their return trip, Nelson slid behind the wheel.

"You're okay driving?" She couldn't disguise the relief in her voice.

He grinned at her. "I'm not exactly in racing form, but I can manage city streets fine."

It took more than half an hour to drive from the airport into town and then locate the downtown address Nelson's friend had supplied him with. He parked in front of a run-down apartment hotel and he and Portia went inside.

The place smelled of tobacco and urine. A bearded man with a belly sat in a rocking chair in the lobby. He pointed at the stairs when they asked for Stuart. "Kid's on the fifth floor, 508, Edgar's place. Elevator's broken. Young folks got better legs than us geezers, so they get the rooms with the view." He cackled and went back to watching a hockey game on the minuscule television mounted high on the wall.

They climbed one steep flight of stairs after another. Nelson could hear Portia's breath coming fast after the first few flights, and he was forced to slow down and rely more and more on the cane as the ache in his hip and feet grew fierce.

They were both panting by the time they reached the fifth floor.

Nelson knocked on 508, and they waited. He knocked again, harder, and after another interval, a key turned and the door opened.

Portia stepped forward. "Hi, Stuart."

"Dr. Portia?" The young man rubbed his eyes with his knuckles as if he thought he was dreaming. He'd obviously been asleep; his hair was sticking up on one side and there was a mark from a ribbed blanket down one cheek. His deep voice was thick and slow.

"How come you're here, Dr. Portia?" His voice took on an excited tone. "Did you bring Juliet with you?" He stepped into the hallway and looked both ways several times. His shoulders slumped when he realized she wasn't there.

"Sorry," Portia said gently. "Juliet isn't here. This is my friend Nelson. It's good to see you again, Stuart." Portia smiled and reached out a hand, and Stuart shook it formally, for a long while. He then took Nelson's hand and did the same.

Nelson hadn't met him before, and he was impressed with the young man's physical condition and the strength of his grip. Stuart wasn't tall, but he was strong. He was wearing an undershirt and a pair of sweat pants, and the muscles on his arms and across his chest were well defined.

"I live here now with my friend Edgar," Stuart said proudly. "My friend Edgar helped me move from Bernice's house. Edgar says I'm an adult. I can live where I want." Stuart rocked from one foot to the other and his brow furrowed. "Bernice and I had a fight. She's real, real mad at me. She's gonna tell my mother on me."

"Edgar's absolutely right. You can live where you want," Portia soothed him. "Good for you for making the decision. Do you think we could come in and talk for a few minutes, Stuart?''

''It's my life. That's what Edgar says. You can come in, sure. Edgar's not home yet. He'll be here at ten-fifteen. He gets off work at ten and then he walks here. He's a janitor. Why didn't Juliet come with you, Portia? I'd really like to see Juliet.''

The apartment was small, dingy and sparsely furnished. It had a combination kitchen-living room, and through an archway Nelson could see into the bedroom, with its narrow twin beds.

Nelson sat on the sagging sofa and Portia chose a battered armchair. There were two posters of sleek, modern cars on the walls and a large picture of Elvis.

Portia plunged right in. ''Did Juliet tell you she was going to have a baby, Stuart?''

His face lit up. ''Our baby. Yup, she told me. That's why I moved from Bernice's house, see, because of our baby. Bernice says no way I could be a father, but I could. I know I could. Bernice took all my money, and I need money for the baby. Edgar helped me bring my stuff here, and I got this good job that I really, really like and I'm saving money. Look.''

He went into the bedroom and returned with a dog-eared bankbook. He handed it proudly to Portia. ''Edgar helped me. He knows all about banks and stuff. I already have eighty-nine bucks. When I have five hundred bucks I'm going to take a bus and get Juliet and bring her here. We can get married and I'll get our own place and a bed for the baby and some clothes and diapers. Juliet already has some clothes for the baby, but they need lots of clothes and diapers, Juliet says. Babies need.''

Nelson had to swallow hard because of the lump in his throat.

"Stuart, there isn't going to be a baby.'' As gently as possible, Portia explained what had happened to Juliet. She went over it twice before Stuart understood, and when he did, he covered his face with his hands and started to weep.

Portia put her arms around him and let him cry it out. "Juliet's asking for you, and we thought maybe you'd want to be with her. Do you want to come back to Vancouver with us now, Stuart, and see Juliet?''

He nodded and sniffled and then blew his nose hard on the tissue Portia handed him. "I want to be with Juliet. I really, really do. But I have to go to work tomorrow. I set the alarm. I can't be late.'' His brow furrowed anew. "And Edgar won't know where I am.''

"I spoke to your boss earlier this evening,'' Nelson said. "How would it be if I called him now and you told him there's been an emergency and you have to go back to Vancouver?''

Stuart thought that over. "Okay. I'll tell him about our baby and tell him I really really need to see Juliet,'' he finally decided. "Juliet needs me.''

"If Edgar gets off work at ten, he should be here soon. And you can explain to him what's happening,'' Portia added.

Stuart's boss was understanding, and at exactly ten-fifteen, the door opened and Edgar entered. He was perhaps forty...tall and thin, with a self-confident air. He eyed Nelson and Portia suspiciously.

"What's goin' on here, buddy? These relatives of yours or somethin'?''

Stuart introduced everyone, and once again Portia related why she and Nelson were there. Clearly Edgar, too, had some form of cognitive impairment, because she had to go over the story several times.

When he finally understood, Edgar gave Stuart an affectionate tap on the shoulder with his fist. "Hey, buddy, sounds like you need to be with your lady. C'mon, I'll help you pack your gear.''

They shoved clothes and toiletries into a backpack. When it came time to leave, the two men hugged awkwardly.

"Stu, you remember what I told ya, now,'' Edgar

instructed. "You gotta live your life your own way. Ya gotta do what ya gotta do."

As a philosophy, Nelson figured it pretty well covered all the bases. Again, he had to swallow hard against the lump in his throat.

The trip back to Vancouver was swift and uneventful. Portia had been concerned about Stuart's reaction to flying, but she should have trusted his fascination with all things mechanical. He asked Nelson one question after another about the small, sleek aircraft, and he was thrilled when Nelson and the pilot showed him the instrument panel and how it worked.

But once they'd landed, it was Juliet he talked about, almost nonstop during the long drive to St. Joe's. There was no doubt about the depth of his feelings for her.

Nelson thought about the enormous courage it had taken for Stuart to move out of his sister's house and assume control of his own life for the first time ever. It had also taken guts to come to Vancouver tonight, and he felt humbled by Stuart's bravery.

When they finally reached the hospital it was almost midnight. A tall, strikingly attractive dark-haired woman met them in the hallway outside Juliet's private room. Nelson could see Portia's patrician features mirrored in this older face, although Lydia's eyes were a clear and piercing emerald instead of smoky gray.

Portia introduced both Stuart and Nelson to her mother, adding a quick explanation about Nelson and the jet.

Stuart held out his hand to Lydia, and when she took it, he pumped it up and down and said, "How do you do, Juliet's mother? I hope you like me, but if you don't, that's okay because I gotta live my life my own way. Is Juliet in that room? 'Cause I need to see her now. I need to see Juliet."

He went in alone and closed the door decisively behind him.

"Well, that's one of the most direct and unusual introductions I've ever had," Lydia remarked after a startled moment. "Let's go sit in that waiting room down the hall. The coffee is abominable, but at least no one's there. I guess everyone's gone to bed except us and the nursing staff."

Her eyes went over Nelson like lasers, and he wondered if her psychic ability included brain scans. "You and I need to get acquainted, Nelson."

He'd intended to leave, but instead he found himself following Lydia down the hall, wondering if this was how a lamb felt being led to the slaughter.

LYDIA'S WORDS SET OFF alarm bells in Portia.

Exactly what was her mother going to say to Nelson? She wasn't noted for her tact. Now Portia wished heartily that she'd never confided in Lydia about her love life. She also wished Nelson would do the polite thing and go on home, where he belonged at this hour. But Portia couldn't exactly accept his help one moment and order him to disappear the next, could she?

Lydia, however, was the soul of discretion. She chatted about racing cars—one of her husbands had owned one—and asked about Nelson's accident. She thanked him for being so helpful tonight, and he mentioned an acquaintance, a retired racing driver, who lived in St. George's and owned a nightclub. It turned out Lydia had been there. They talked about other clubs they'd visited, until Portia's head started to ache.

She debated the dangers of leaving them alone together and decided to chance them. "I think I'll go see how Stuart and Juliet are doing."

The door was still closed. Portia opened it an inch and peeked inside. Stuart was sitting on the bed, holding Juliet's hands between both of his. She was propped up on pillows; her face and his were wet with tears.

"Hey, guys, can I come in?"

Portia went over and hugged her sister. It was Stuart who spoke first.

"We're gonna get married," he said in a no-nonsense tone. "We're gonna get married today."

"Tomorrow, Stuart," Juliet corrected him. "Remember the doctor said I can go home tomorrow, in the morning, so we can get married in the afternoon. Right, Portia?"

"You can't stop us, either," Stuart added, giving Portia a belligerent look. "Nobody can."

Portia smiled at him. "Oh, Stuart, I wouldn't want to stop you. I think it's wonderful. Congratulations."

"I told you Portia would be happy for us. I told you so," Juliet said, giving her sister a wide, watery grin that faded as another thought struck her.

"Where's our mother? Did she go back to the hotel?"

"Of course not. She's just down the hall, and she'll be thrilled to hear about your plans. She loves weddings. Look at how many she's had herself," Portia pointed out, adding with just the barest touch of malice, "I'll bet she'll arrange everything for you, just the way you want it." That would keep Lydia busy for the rest of her short stay.

And their mother could also sort out just exactly where Stuart and Juliet were planning to live, Portia decided. If it was Seattle, it would involve a major amount of reorganizing. These two certainly couldn't live with Edgar. They were going to need a lot of counseling.

"Portia, I can't have any more ba—bies," Juliet's face crumpled. "The doctor came and told me." Her woebegone expression was heartbreaking.

"I know, honey," Portia said. "I'm so sorry." She held her sister close and let her grieve. But there was no point in dwelling on the sadness. "Look, I'll go get Mother and you can tell her what kind of wedding you want."

Lydia and Nelson were deep in conversation when Portia came through the door. Lydia broke off in midsentence.

"They're getting married tomorrow," Portia announced, dying to know what Lydia had been saying. "They want you to arrange the wedding, Mother."

Lydia flopped back in her chair and rolled her eyes. "Tomorrow? That's impossible. I'd need at least a week. Your brothers won't be able to make it unless they have some notice, and neither will Malcolm. You'd better go and talk some sense into them, dear."

Portia didn't move and forced herself not to say anything.

Lydia gave Portia a look, sighed and then got to her feet. "All right, I'll go myself. I've enjoyed talking with you, Nelson. And of course you'll attend the wedding."

It was a statement instead of a question, and Nelson nodded agreement. "Absolutely. I'd be honored."

Portia would cheerfully have strangled her mother. Surely Lydia could guess how painful it was for her to be around Nelson. And having him at the wedding would be agonizing, for God's sake. Her mother had all the sensitivity of a gerbil.

Nelson waited until Lydia was gone and then said, "Unless you'd rather I didn't come, Portia?"

She struggled with honesty and lost. "Of course you should come," she lied. After all, he'd been instrumental in finding Stuart and bringing him here. Portia wasn't mean-spirited enough to tell him to stay away from the wedding.

"Besides, Jules will want you there." That, at least, was the truth. Juliet loved Nelson. Maybe it was a genetic flaw in the Bailey women, because even Lydia had seemed charmed by him.

"I'll be seeing you soon, then, Doc." He touched her cheek with a fingertip, hardly a touch at all, but it burned like fire on her skin. "I'll just go in and ask Stuart if he wants to bunk with me tonight. He'll need a place to stay until the wedding. Maybe a little male bonding won't hurt either of us." He smiled and winked, and her heart gave a familiar thump.

"'Night, Portia."

"Good night. And thank you."

She'd assumed Stuart would come home with her,

and she couldn't pretend even to herself that she'd looked forward to it. She'd been on an emotional roller coaster all day, and she needed to be alone for a while, get some sleep. Nelson knew that, and he was making it easier for her. Why did he have to be so damn thoughtful? Blast the man, why couldn't he just be a jerk? That would make it so much easier to get over him.

A glance at her watch showed it was nearly two in the morning, but there was one more stop she had to make before she headed home. She'd promised Cedric.

The Palliative Care Unit was hushed and dimly lit. She wasn't about to disturb him at this hour, but she couldn't relax without assuring herself that he was resting as comfortably as possible.

She found a nurse at the station, and the moment she said Cedric's name, Portia knew. The nurse's colors trumpeted the answer even before she spoke.

"I guess you didn't get my message, Dr. Bailey. I left it on your machine. Mr. Vencouer died at 10: 43 this evening. Gordon Caldwell was with him. The covering physician, Dr. Gallatly, signed the certificate. I called the central registry to notify them of consent for donation of corneas. Will you be wanting an autopsy?"

"No, no autopsy." Portia felt numb.

"The body's gone to the morgue. Mr. Vencouer had you and Mr. Nelson Gregory listed on the admission form as next of kin. I was unable to reach Mr. Gregory, either. I left a message at his home number. We need to know where to release the body.''

Portia was stunned. She'd assumed Cedric had spoken with Gordon about what he wanted done when he died. Instead, he'd named her and Nelson next of kin, realizing it would force them to cooperate.

''I'll—I'll contact Mr. Gregory and we'll notify you of the arrangements in the morning.''

Cedric, how could you do this to me?

She heard his voice in her mind's ear, the way it had sounded before he got sick, that strong, musical tenor: *None ever was so fair as I thought you...*

He'd loved her. He'd wanted her to have her heart's desire, and he'd known all too well what that was. And so he'd done the only thing he could do to bring her and Nelson together.

Oh, my dear, beloved friend. Thank you for trying, but it isn't going to work.

She made it out of the hospital before the tears began.

CHAPTER SEVENTEEN

NELSON COULDN'T SLEEP. He tried to blame the quantities of pizza and beer he and Stuart had consumed before they headed for bed, but it wasn't that. Strangely enough, neither was it the familiar worry over the results of the test.

It could have something to do with his conversation with Lydia. The moment Portia left, her mother had stopped the polite chitchat and gone for his jugular, just as he'd known she would.

"Portia told me all about you," Lydia had said. "I'll make this fast, because she'll be back soon. I've never seen her as unhappy as she is right now, and I blame you. It's not up to anyone else to make us happy. It's our own responsibility. But where love's concerned, we do have an obligation. You're in love with my daughter. Do I have that part right?"

"Yes, you do." Nelson could feel his temper rising. He didn't want or need a lecture from this haughty woman. His voice grew soft and steely. "I assume she told you about the Huntington's. Obviously I have to find out the test results before I can make any plans for my life or for hers.''

Lydia snorted. ''That's a load of rubbish. She told me you don't have the disease, and I believe her. It seems to me that if you truly loved my daughter, you'd trust her on this one, Nelson.'' Lydia leaned toward him, accusing and passionate. ''And so what if you did get it? She doesn't need happily ever after, and what makes you think you could promise her that anyway? All any woman wants is unconditional love *at this moment*. If you wait until the test results come, you'll lose her.''

The words echoed in Nelson's brain. He punched the pillow, and outrage surged through him. What was it with these damn women? His own mother, then Portia, now Lydia, all insisting that doing the sensible, mature thing was a mistake. The irony was that he'd lived on the edge for years, risking his life in ways that would make their hair stand on end. Yet when it came to emotions, they were the ones advocating risk.

He flopped onto his back, and for the first time, he admitted to himself that dangerous sports no longer appealed to him. He'd started flying lessons, but he had no real desire to go on with them. Neither did he long to get back on the racetrack. He hadn't yet figured out what he'd do to fill in the time he used to fill with danger, but something would come to him.

He'd changed; love had changed him.

Portia had changed him. The fact that Stuart was at this moment asleep in his spare bedroom was just one example of how she'd broadened his life and his attitudes.

Before Portia, he would have avoided Stuart. He'd have felt awkward and nervous in his presence; he'd never have been able to laugh with him and drink beer and eat pizza and feel absolutely at ease, even fond of the other man, as he had tonight.

He'd never have met or gotten to know Cedric, either. How he admired Cedric's ability to get beyond jealousy, because of course Cedric was in love with Portia, too. Nelson applauded the man's taste in women, and felt humbled and awed by his raw courage in the face of death.

But he didn't want to think about death.

The bed was a tangle of sheets, and his nerves were jumping. Sleep was impossible. He gave up and swung his legs to the floor. Once he found his cane, he limped to the kitchen and took a bottle of water out of the fridge. The message light on the phone was blinking. He'd noticed it earlier and ignored it; now he reached out to activate the tape.

"Nelson, I can't sleep." Stuart's loud, plaintive

voice startled him. He almost dropped the water, and he forgot about the machine.

"I'm scared for the wedding, Nelson." Stuart's face was screwed into a worried knot. "They ask you things when you get married. You have to say stuff. I saw it on television. And I won't know what to say when they ask me. Juliet knows, but I don't." His chin wobbled. "Everybody will laugh at me."

"No, they won't, sport." Nelson changed his mind about the water and put on a pot of coffee, instead. "Fact is, I don't know them myself. So we'll look the things up and go over them until we both know them off by heart." He unearthed a prayer book from his bookshelves, and for the rest of the night he and Stuart practiced reciting the wedding vows to each other.

By 6:00 a.m., they were both letter-perfect. Stuart finally staggered off to his room, confident that he'd make it through the ceremony, and Nelson collapsed on the sofa, too weary even to head for the bedroom. Witnessing Stuart's struggle to memorize his lines had been exhausting.

God, the kid had guts. Stuart and Cedric had that in common. They took the sucker punches life dealt them and did what they could without whining. A guy could learn one hell of a lot from those two.

Nelson closed his eyes, on the verge of sleep, and then, as if a locked door suddenly slammed open when he tried the handle one last time, he finally got it. The shock was so great he stumbled to his feet, heart pumping.

Stuart and Cedric accepted the way they were, *right now*. They *lived* right now; they didn't wait.

What the hell was it Lydia had said?

All any woman wants is unconditional love *at this moment*. His mother had told him the same thing, in different words. Portia had tried to make him understand, and he hadn't heard her.

God, he'd been a deaf and blind fool. He'd wasted so much time, so many precious hours, so many irreplaceable days.

He wouldn't waste one more minute. He grabbed his cane and hurried to the phone. Portia answered on the first ring, which surprised him. He'd thought she'd be sleeping. Instead, she sounded wide awake, and she'd been crying. She *was* crying.

He'd spent the night rehearsing a wedding. His heart sank as she told him he was about to spend a day planning a funeral. The news of Cedric's death brought a lump to his throat, but it also reinforced his decision.

Before another hour of his own life had a chance to fly past, Nelson was going to propose to the woman he loved.

PORTIA OPENED THE DOOR when Nelson rang. She knew she looked about as bad as it was possible to look, and she felt about the same. She'd slept only an hour or two. She couldn't seem to stop crying. Her eyes were swollen; her nose, red; her robe, the old and tattered plaid her father had given her for her sixteenth birthday. She was having some sort of breakdown; she hadn't worn the robe since her intern days, and she hardly ever thought about her father.

Nelson, on the other hand, was freshly shaved and showered, in clean jeans, white sweatshirt, tan leather bomber jacket. She was too depleted even to feel a speck of resentment toward him for being perfectly groomed at 6:45 in the morning.

Seeing him just made her feel sad, and the familiar burning began behind her eyes. She tried to hold back, but the bitter tears started all over again. She mopped at them with the back of her hand and sniffled.

"Ah, Portia. Don't cry, sweetheart." He stepped inside and tried to take her in his arms.

She had just enough sense of self-preservation to move back, out of his reach. "I'll make a fresh pot of coffee." She'd already had a pot on her own, and she felt light-headed and spacey from it. She hurried toward the kitchen, grabbing a tissue en route.

"I don't know what's wrong with me. I've had patients die before," she said in a reasonable tone, blowing her nose hard. "I called Gordon. Cedric's left all the directions for his funeral, but he wants you and me to carry them out." In spite of herself, her voice rose to a wail. "Why couldn't he just have let Gordon do it? I'd really rather not be around you, Nelson."

There, she'd said it. She turned her back on him and reached into the cupboard for the coffee.

"I'm sorry you feel that way."

She could feel the warmth of his breath on the back of her neck. She jerked and turned. He was standing right behind her. His arms were on either side of her, resting on the counter, trapping her. His face was inches away. He'd used peppermint toothpaste. She hadn't even brushed her teeth yet. It was just one more confirmation of the insurmountable differences between them.

"I'm so sorry I've hurt you, Portia. I never intended to do that, because I love you with all my heart."

Her heart was pounding like a kettledrum and she wondered if she was having cardiac arrhythmia. Too much caffeine, she reminded herself. Too much emotion, too much Nelson, too early in the morning.

"Step back from the counter, please." God, she sounded like a cop.

He did, but then he dropped to one knee on the

tile floor. Her first thought was that his injured foot had given way.

"Portia, will you marry me?"

She waited for the qualifying part, the *if* and *when,* but the silence lengthened. At last she figured it out. "You got the test results. I *told* you you didn't have it."

"Nope. They're not due for another three weeks."

She frowned down at him. "So why are you asking me this now?"

"Because—I—love—you."

A warm, fuzzy feeling began in her chest, but she squelched it. It was far too soon to take anything for granted. "What about the Huntington's?"

"You said I don't have it. If you're wrong, you'll just have to take your chances."

"And you're sure about this?"

"Damn it, Portia, I've never been as sure of anything in my life. I wouldn't be down here in this ridiculous position on these hard tiles if I wasn't sure." He was losing patience; she could see it in the tightening of his jaw. His hip was probably starting to hurt.

She still wasn't ready to believe. "When?"

"Portia, *please.* When, what?"

"When do you want us to get married?" She just knew he was going to say three weeks, after the test results came back, and she'd be right back where she'd started from, only worse.

"Today. Tomorrow. I don't care. The sooner the better."

Something that felt like bubbles started pulsing through her arteries.

"Okay, then. But we should arrange the funeral first." She felt a stab of guilt. "Do you think it's disrespectful to Cedric, talking about a wedding at the same time we're planning his funeral?"

Nelson was on his feet, and his arms were around her, holding her so tight her ribs were in danger of cracking. "I think he's up there opening a bottle of champagne and toasting us right now."

CEDRIC HAD TOLD GORDON exactly what he wanted. The service was simple and straightforward, held in St. Joe's chapel, conducted by the hospital chaplain, attended by four of Cedric's street friends, the palliative care personnel who'd gotten to know him during his stay and Nelson, Portia and Gordon.

Cedric had asked that a few lines from Shakespeare be read. He'd marked for Gordon the ones he wanted in his well-worn volume, *Shakespeare Complete*. He'd requested that his ashes be scattered on the ocean at sunset.

"'Let me not to the marriage of true minds admit impediments,'" Gordon read aloud as the service ended. "'Love is not love that alters when it alteration finds, or bends with the remover to remove. Oh, no, it is an ever-fixed mark, that looks on tempests and is never shaken. It is the star to every wandering bark, whose worth's unknown although his height be taken.'"

Portia was crying again, but this time the tears were gentle, a benediction and an acknowledgment to and from Cedric. He'd chosen one other piece of poetry that spoke of death in literary terms, but Portia knew this final quote was Cedric's parting gift to her and to Nelson.

THREE DAYS LATER Juliet and Portia had a double wedding, a candlelight ceremony held on Thursday evening in the little side chapel of a west-side church. There was a Christmas tree in the corner, and the smell of evergreen and beeswax mingled with the perfume and aftershave of the small group of guests.

Lydia, with Joanne's help, had performed miracles in a few short days. The altar and the sides of the aisle were heaped with dozens of poinsettias and huge bouquets of white and red roses. Lydia had found Juliet a long velvet dress in purple, the color Juliet wanted to be married in. It was empire style, and Lydia fastened a garland of pink rosebuds in her daughter's hair, to match the bouquet she carried.

Portia wore a draped silver silk jersey dress she'd seen months before in a boutique window and bought on impulse. She'd never found exactly the right occasion to wear it, till now. Her bouquet was lily of the valley and freesia, and Joanne had pinned some of the blossoms in Portia's dark hair.

Portia walked down the aisle hand in hand with her sister to the strains of Handel's *Water Music*. Juliet's fingers were entwined with Portia's, and Portia couldn't tell whether her own fingers trembled or Juliet's.

She saw Lydia's husband, Malcolm, smiling at them from the front pew where he sat beside their mother. He'd flown in late the night before to attend the ceremony, and he'd given the brides the double strands of pearls that encircled their throats. One of Portia's brothers, Antony, had also managed to come, and he shot his sisters a grin and gave them a thumbs-up.

Nelson and Stuart were waiting at the altar, both perfectly tailored, Stuart in dark gray, Nelson in black. Both wore white shirts. Portia noticed that Nelson's tie was maroon, Stuart's floral.

She loosened Juliet's hand and took her place beside the man she loved. The ceremony began, performed by a round, motherly pastor whose smile never wavered and whose composure was admirable, even when one of the guests from Harmony House, overcome with excitement, burst into a chorus of "Jingle Bells" during the exchange of vows.

When Nelson hesitated slightly during the exchange of vows, Stuart prompted him in a loud whisper.

Portia knew she herself must have repeated the age-old covenant, but she wasn't conscious of having done so, not then, not afterward.

All she remembered was the magnificent colors blazing around him, colors that she recognized as passion, joy, generosity, confidence. And endless, boundless, unlimited love.

She saw that love shining in Nelson's eyes as he slid the ring on her finger, and she felt it on his lips when the pastor said, "You may now kiss the bride."

EPILOGUE

THEY LAUGHED THEIR WAY through a fast number, and then the music slowed. It swirled around them, soft and romantic, and he drew her close.

Portia floated in Nelson's arms, and he thought how well they danced together, like one organism whose four limbs moved in perfect synchronicity. His hip ached like fury, but exercise was good for it.

"This has physical therapy beat to hell," he murmured in her ear. "And I'll bet it's like sex. The more we do it..."

She rolled her eyes and laughed with him. His breath caught in his throat at her beauty, at the amazing fact that she was his wife.

He'd planned every detail of this evening. It was their third anniversary. They'd been married three weeks.

He'd hired Charlie to chauffeur them around. They'd had dinner at the restaurant where they'd first eaten together, and then he'd brought her here to Flashbacks, to dance.

She'd forgotten the tickets he'd given her so long ago, the promise he'd made to waltz the night away with her in his arms. He hadn't. The surprise and pleasure on her face when they walked into the popular club had delighted him.

The medley ended and he led her back to the table. The band took a break. Nelson had ordered a bottle of champagne, and now he poured them each a glass.

"To your new job," he toasted. The week after their wedding, she'd met with the doctors starting the clinic that specialized in alternative medicine. They'd offered her a job, and she'd accepted. The clinic would open in two weeks, and Portia would be there, using her psychic abilities instead of trying to ignore them.

"Is that what you're so excited about?" Portia sipped her wine and gave him that look, the one that he'd come to recognize. She was seeing his colors. He couldn't get away with a damn thing around her. He pulled the envelope out of his pocket and slid it across the table to her.

"What's this?"

"It's my mission statement," he teased. The envelope held copies of the ad material he'd had drawn up as a first step toward starting his new career as a business consultant. It would run in major magazines, and he was excited about it.

She opened it, glanced at the photo and then at the copy, and grinned. The picture of him had been taken just before a race, although he wasn't recognizable. He was climbing into the Ferrari, wearing a padded blue jumpsuit and a crash helmet. The copy read; "With Gregory as your business consultant, no way are you heading down the same old road. Courage to innovate, skill to execute."

"It's perfect, Nelson. I love it." Her eyes telegraphed that she loved him, too. "Did you talk to Bernardo about the zippers?"

"He's making up samples. We'll take them to rehab places and see what happens."

"Charlie and her limo, Bernardo and his zippers. Your first customers are a result of your accident. But Joanne always says there aren't any accidents in life, that everything's for a purpose."

"She's right." He pulled another envelope out and handed it to her. "This came today." It was from the Department of Genetics at the university. "You were right, too, Portia. I don't have it. Our kids won't have it, either." It was a peculiarity of Huntington's. If he had inherited it, their children would have had a fifty percent chance of inheriting it from him. Because the genetic weakness wasn't present in him, their children weren't at risk.

Her eyes widened, and then glimmered with tears. "I won't say I told you so." The smile she gave him was luminous. She lifted her glass and toasted him. ''Here's to the gift of time.''

He looked at her and wished there were a bigger word for love.

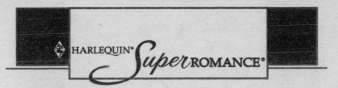

Welcome to Montana

Home of the Rocky Mountains, Yellowstone National Park, slow-moving glaciers and the spectacular Going to the Sun Highway.

Set against this unforgettable background, Harlequin Superromance introduces the **Maxwells of Montana**—a family that's lived and ranched here for generations.

You won't want to miss this brand-new trilogy— three exciting romances by three of your favorite authors.

MARRIED IN MONTANA
by Lynnette Kent on sale August 2001

A MONTANA FAMILY
by Roxanne Rustand on sale September 2001

MY MONTANA HOME
by Ellen James on sale October 2001

Available wherever Harlequin books are sold.

HARLEQUIN®
Makes any time special ®

Harlequin truly does make any time special. . . . This year we are celebrating weddings in style!

To help us celebrate, we want you to tell us how wearing the Harlequin wedding gown will make your wedding day special. As the grand prize, Harlequin will offer one lucky bride the chance to **"Walk Down the Aisle"** in the Harlequin wedding gown!

There's more...

For her honeymoon, she and her groom will spend five nights at the **Hyatt Regency Maui.** As part of this five-night honeymoon at the hotel renowned for its romantic attractions, the couple will enjoy a candlelit dinner for two in Swan Court, a sunset sail on the hotel's catamaran, and duet spa treatments.

To enter, please write, in, 250 words or less, how wearing the Harlequin wedding gown will make your wedding day special. The entry will be judged based on its emotionally compelling nature, its originality and creativity, and its sincerity. This contest is open to Canadian and U.S. residents only and to those who are 18 years of age and older. There is no purchase necessary to enter. Void where prohibited. See further contest rules attached. Please send your entry to:

Walk Down the Aisle Contest

In Canada	In U.S.A.
P.O. Box 637	P.O. Box 9076
Fort Erie, Ontario	3010 Walden Ave.
L2A 5X3	Buffalo, NY 14269-9076

You can also enter by visiting www.eHarlequin.com

Win the Harlequin wedding gown and the vacation of a lifetime!
The deadline for entries is October 1, 2001.

1. To enter, follow directions published in the offer to which you are responding. Contest begins April 2, 2001, and ends on October 1, 2001. Method of entry may vary. Mailed entries must be postmarked by October 1, 2001, and received by October 8, 2001.

2. Contest entry may be, at times, presented via the Internet, but will be restricted solely to residents of certain geographic areas that are disclosed on the Web site. To enter via the Internet, if permissible, access the Harlequin Web site (www.eHarlequin.com) and follow the directions displayed online. Online entries must be received by 11:59 p.m. E.S.T. on October 1, 2001.

   In lieu of submitting an entry online, enter by mail by hand-printing (or typing) on an 8½" x 11" plain piece of paper, your name, address (including zip code), Contest number/name and in 250 words or fewer, why winning a Harlequin wedding dress would make your wedding day special. Mail via first-class mail to: Harlequin Walk Down the Aisle Contest 1197, (in the U.S.) P.O. Box 9076, 3010 Walden Avenue, Buffalo, NY 14269-9076, (in Canada) P.O. Box 637, Fort Erie, Ontario L2A 5X3, Canada.

   Limit one entry per person, household address and e-mail address. Online and/or mailed entries received from persons residing in geographic areas in which Internet entry is not permissible will be disqualified.

3. Contests will be judged by a panel of members of the Harlequin editorial, marketing and public relations staff based on the following criteria:

   • Originality and Creativity—50%
   • Emotionally Compelling—25%
   • Sincerity—25%

   In the event of a tie, duplicate prizes will be awarded. Decisions of the judges are final.

4. All entries become the property of Torstar Corp. and will not be returned. No responsibility is assumed for lost, late, illegible, incomplete, inaccurate, nondelivered or misdirected mail or misdirected e-mail, for technical, hardware or software failures of any kind, lost or unavailable network connections, or failed, incomplete, garbled or delayed computer transmission or any human error which may occur in the receipt or processing of the entries in this Contest.

5. Contest open only to residents of the U.S. (except Puerto Rico) and Canada, who are 18 years of age or older, and is void wherever prohibited by law; all applicable laws and regulations apply. Any litigation within the Province of Quebec respecting the conduct or organization of a publicity contest may be submitted to the Régie des alcools, des courses et des jeux for a ruling. Any litigation respecting the awarding of a prize may be submitted to the Régie des alcools, des courses et des jeux only for the purpose of helping the parties reach a settlement. Employees and immediate family members of Torstar Corp. and D. L. Blair, Inc., their affiliates, subsidiaries and all other agencies, entities and persons connected with the use, marketing or conduct of this Contest are not eligible to enter. Taxes on prizes are the sole responsibility of winners. Acceptance of any prize offered constitutes permission to use winner's name, photograph or other likeness for the purposes of advertising, trade and promotion on behalf of Torstar Corp., its affiliates and subsidiaries without further compensation to the winner, unless prohibited by law.

6. Winners will be determined no later than November 15, 2001, and will be notified by mail. Winners will be required to sign and return an Affidavit of Eligibility form within 15 days after winner notification. Noncompliance within that time period may result in disqualification and an alternative winner may be selected. Winners of trip must execute a Release of Liability prior to ticketing and must possess required travel documents (e.g. passport, photo ID) where applicable. Trip must be completed by November 2002. No substitution of prize permitted by winner. Torstar Corp. and D. L. Blair, Inc., their parents, affiliates, and subsidiaries are not responsible for errors in printing or electronic presentation of Contest, entries and/or game pieces. In the event of printing or other errors which may result in unintended prize values or duplication of prizes, all affected game pieces or entries shall be null and void. If for any reason the Internet portion of the Contest is not capable of running as planned, including infection by computer virus, bugs, tampering, unauthorized intervention, fraud, technical failures, or any other causes beyond the control of Torstar Corp. which corrupt or affect the administration, secrecy, fairness, integrity or proper conduct of the Contest, Torstar Corp. reserves the right, at its sole discretion, to disqualify any individual who tampers with the entry process and to cancel, terminate, modify or suspend the Contest or the Internet portion thereof. In the event of a dispute regarding an online entry, the entry will be deemed submitted by the authorized holder of the e-mail account submitted at the time of entry. Authorized account holder is defined as the natural person who is assigned to an e-mail address by an Internet access provider, online service provider or other organization that is responsible for arranging e-mail address for the domain associated with the submitted e-mail address. **Purchase or acceptance of a product offer does not improve your chances of winning.**

7. Prizes: (1) Grand Prize—A Harlequin wedding dress (approximate retail value: $3,500) and a 5-night/6-day honeymoon trip to Maui, HI, including round-trip air transportation provided by Maui Visitors Bureau from Los Angeles International Airport (winner is responsible for transportation to and from Los Angeles International Airport) and a Harlequin Romance Package, including hotel accomodations (double occupancy) at the Hyatt Regency Maui Resort and Spa, dinner for (2) two at Swan Court, a sunset sail on Kiele V and a spa treatment for the winner (approximate retail value: $4,000); (5) Five runner-up prizes of a $1000 gift certificate to selected retail outlets to be determined by Sponsor (retail value $1000 ea.). Prizes consist of only those items listed as part of the prize. Limit one prize per person. All prizes are valued in U.S. currency.

8. For a list of winners (available after December 17, 2001) send a self-addressed, stamped envelope to: Harlequin Walk Down the Aisle Contest 1197 Winners, P.O. Box 4200 Blair, NE 68009-4200 or you may access the www.eHarlequin.com Web site through January 15, 2002.

Contest sponsored by Torstar Corp., P.O. Box 9042, Buffalo, NY 14269-9042, U.S.A.

PHWDACONT2

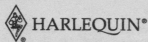

COMING SOON...

AN EXCITING
OPPORTUNITY TO SAVE
ON THE PURCHASE OF
HARLEQUIN AND
SILHOUETTE BOOKS!

*DETAILS TO FOLLOW
IN OCTOBER 2001!*

YOU WON'T WANT TO MISS IT!

PHQ401